PRAISE FOR CORINNA TURNER'S BOOKS

PRAISE FOR *ELFLING*

I was instantly drawn in

EOIN COLFER, author of *Artemis Fowl* and former Irish Children's Laureate

PRAISE FOR THE UNSPARKED SERIES

What a terrifying futuristic world Turner has created!
I am a huge fan of this author and am always impressed with how different all her stories are. Look forward to the next one in this series!

LESLEA WAHL, author of award-winning *The Perfect Blindside*

A cross between Jurassic World *and* Mad Max!
Fun, fast paced. And sets up an incredible new world.
I read it three times in two days!

STEVEN R. MCEVOY, BookReviewsAndMore Blogger and Amazon Top 500 Reviewer

Wow! So suspenseful you won't be able to put it down!

KATY HUTH JONES, author of *Treachery and Truth*

A fun read! Great tension ...
Jurassic Park *fans will love this short!*

CAROLYN ASTFALK, author of *Rightfully Ours*

Very short, but extremely exciting. ... The action is brutal, but it drags you in and doesn't let you go until you hit the last page.
ASHLEY STANGL

ALSO BY CORINNA TURNER:

I AM MARGARET series
For older teens and up

Brothers *(A Prequel Novella)**
1: I Am Margaret*
1: Io Sono Margaret (Italian)
2: The Three Most Wanted*
3: Liberation*
4: Bane's Eyes*
5: Margo's Diary*
6: The Siege of Reginald Hill*
7: A Saint in the Family*
'The Underappreciated Virtues of Rusty
Old Bicycles' *(Prequel short story) Also
found in the anthology:*
Secrets: Visible & Invisible*

I Am Margaret: The Play (*Adapted by
Fiorella de Maria*)

UNSPARKED series
For tweens and up

Main Series:
1: Please Don't Feed the Dinosaurs*
2: A Truly Raptor-ous Welcome
3: PANIC!*
4: Farmgirls Die in Cages*
5: Wild Life
6: A Right Rex Rodeo
7: FEAR
8: A Different Kind of Camouflage
9: A Different Kind of Freedom
10: What's Done is Done†

Prequels:
BREACH!*
A Mom With Blue Feathers†
A Very Jurassic Christmas*
'Liam and the Hunters of Lee'Vi'
'A Truly Clawful Christmas'

FRIENDS IN HIGH PLACES series
For tweens and up

1: The Boy Who Knew (Carlo Acutis)*
2: Old Men Don't Walk to Egypt (Saint
Joseph)*
3: Child, Unwanted (Margaret of
Castello)*

Do Carpenter's Dream of Wooden
Sheep? *(Spin-off, comes between 1 & 2)*

1: El Chico Que Lo Sabia (Spanish)
1: Il Ragazzo Che Sapeva (Italian)

YESTERDAY & TOMORROW series
For adults and mature teens only
Someday: A Novella*
Eines Tages (German)
1: Tomorrow's Dead†

OTHER WORKS

For teens and up
Elfling*
'The Most Expensive Alley Cat in London'
(Elfling *prequel short story*)

For tweens and up
Mandy Lamb & The Full Moon*
The Wolf, The Lamb, and The Air Balloon
(Mandy Lamb *novella*)

For adults and new adults
Three Last Things *or* The Hounding of Carl
Jarrold, Soulless Assassin*
A Changing of the Guard*

The Raven & The Yew†

† **Coming Soon**
* **Awarded the Catholic Writers Guild** *Seal of Approval*

2

A TRULY RAPTOR-OUS WELCOME

CORINNA TURNER

unSeen

A TRULY RAPTOR-OUS WELCOME

CORINNA TURNER

DARRYL

A roar of challenge from an edmontosaur brings me fully awake. Raptors bothering the calves? I listen for a few minutes. A rumble...more of a grumble...from another edmo. Ah, just two mares vying for dominance within our herd.

Early morning silence falls again. Automatically, the first thing I do every morning, I glance at the ScreamerBand on my wrist—the light glows green. No power loss to our electric fence in the night; no alarms tripped. All safe and secure. Only the barest hint of daylight manages to filter in past the strong steel shutters, and I snuggle down in my bed, yawning. It's just past six, and I don't need to be up until six-thirty.

I'm wide awake, though. No point staying in bed. I can get my chores done early and—

Ooooh! Carol! I'd forgotten. My new step-mom is here. Her first day on the Franklyn farm. Yes, if I get done quickly, I can be around to help her settle in. After that awful journey yesterday—the closest we've ever come to being eaten by raptors!—she could probably use some TLC.

Dressing quickly in work clothes, I brush and braid my shoulder-length brown hair, pull my rifle from under the bed and head downstairs. First stop, House Control, where I check all the readings carefully. Normally Dad gets up before everyone and drives the fence, but I'm pretty sure he's sleeping-in this morning, though my mind shies away from why. Our twin Renfield Ozone 4 is a very good fence, anyway— we can occasionally go out before he's inspected it without any concern. Not so long as all the readings are okay, and there's certainly no sign of the slightest overnight disturbance or malfunction. I can put my rifle away for the day.

I press the button to open the downstairs shutters—better leave the upstairs ones or I'll wake Dad and Carol and Harry. Though Harry might already be up. Despite now being technically a teenager, he's got no more patience for lying around in bed than I have, though I'm three years older than him.

Light spills into the hall as the shutters snick back. I turn towards the gun locker, glancing out of the window by the door.

What's that?

Stepping closer, I peer outside. My blood goes cold through every vein, like it's been freeze-dried.

There in a patch of mud are two footprints.

An almost three-toed pad mark with the third toe print missing.

Unmistakeable.

I leap for the House Control, slamming my hand on the shutter button. As they close again, I'm already grabbing my ScreamerBand, pressing the alarm.

Oh God, don't let Harry have gone out already! Please?

"Harry? *Harry?*" The breach alarm blasts through the house and shrieks from the band on my own wrist as I take the stairs four at a time. "*Harry?*"

I hurtle towards his door and almost collide with him as he opens it, his rifle in his hands.

"Darryl? What—?"

"Harry, thank God! We've got raptor prints in the yard!"

I spin and leap for the ladder up to our turret. Harry swears and follows.

The sound of Dad's door opening.

"Raptor prints in the yard," I hear Harry relay to Dad.

I check the panel by the turret hatch, but all is well inside, the video screen empty of threat and no alarms triggered. Not entirely reassuring this morning, since no alarms have been triggered anywhere else either.

Unfastening the hatch, I cautiously push it up. The lights come on, and the turret is as empty as it's supposed to be. I scramble up and press the button to raise the turret's shutters, though not its raptor-proof windows, hitting the 'mute' button on the breach alarm so I can hear.

The farm lies spread out around us, peaceful in the soft morning light. The barns, gathered around the yard, the road leading through our mammal-stock

3

pastures to the gate. Everything still and calm, except for the eye-watering glare flickering across the scene—the strobe on the breach siren mounted on a pole above the turret continues to flash even though no longer making that awful racket. An unseen signal will have gone out to the neighboring farms, alerting them to our predicament.

I double-check the camera sound is switched on...yep. Normal early morning sounds. I switch the audio to the inside of one of the mammal-stock barns—if a raptor is prowling outside they'll know.

A soft low. A faint rustle of straw. The usual sounds of calm cows at daybreak. I switch the audio quickly to the next barn, then the next. The mammal-stock are all unconcerned.

"So, where are you?" I whisper, looking out of the windows again.

"Yo, where is it?" Harry climbs up into the turret, his green eyes—so like Mom's—wide under his tousled brown hair. From excitement, rather than fear, since his lightly tanned skin is a normal pink-beige color.

"I haven't found any sign of it yet. Other than the footprints. Where's Dad?"

"He's got his hands full with Lettuce Lady."

I snort, then try to make up for it with a disapproving look. "I thought we were going to give her a chance to adjust?"

"Yeah, sorry. I think I hurtled out the wrong side of the bed when the breach alarm woke me from a nice dream."

"Yeah, well, you take the windows, I'll take the monitors."

I start to work my way around the little screens on the console ledge that rings the turret, which display the feed from the cameras located all over the farm, anywhere that's not line of sight from here. On one of them we should glimpse our uninvited guest. Harry moves behind me, like my shadow, only he's looking out through the windows, his eyes searching for a leathery face or feathery tail.

Where are you?

"Anything?" Harry asks rather unnecessarily, when we've made the full circle.

"Nothing. Let's swap and go again."

We make the circuit again, with me scanning the view from the windows and Harry checking the monitors.

"Still nothing!" I slap a hand on the console ledge in frustration, then quickly flick through the audio from the barns again. Everything on the farm is calm and happy—except us.

"Hey, kids?" Dad finally arrives at the base of the ladder, peering up with eyes as blue as my own. "What is it and where is it?"

"Dakotaraptor, well-grown, probably male, from the pugmarks," I call back. "But where? We can't spot it anywhere, Dad!"

"Let me see." Dad reaches for the ladder, but pauses to detach a pair of elegant, clutching arms. "Come on, honey, I've got to go up there for a minute. Soon as we deal with this we can have some breakfast, hmm?"

"Breakfast?" The whimper comes from out of sight—it sounds as though Carol is so far from being interested in breakfast right now she can hardly remember what the word means.

When Dad makes it up the ladder at last, breathing a little deeply from using the shoulder that got clawed yesterday, but making no sound of pain, I add, "Mammal-stock are all fine. No signs of nervousness."

"Huh. That's weird. They should be telling us exactly where the critter is."

"I know; it's the first thing I tried."

"Could it have, like, come in at night, prowled around a bit and got out again?" suggests Harry.

"It simply should not be possible for it to get in at all, let alone get in and out again," says Dad, now busy scanning the screens. "But not having seen how it got in, we can't rule it out entirely. Right, I can't spot it either. Let's get the drone up and check the fence."

He moves to a set of controls on the console and we hear the clank-click as the drone dome on top of the turret slides open and the drone is released. We watch the drone's screen closely as Dad makes a quick sweep of the farm buildings, then heads for the fence.

Still no sign of Mr. Raptor.

"Come on!" Dad's almost snarling, though under his breath. "Come on, where are you, you blasted *outage!*"

I exchange looks with Harry. Dad doesn't usually swear in front of us. He's furious—dismayed?—to have something like this happen on Carol's first day, especially after the near-fatal fiasco yesterday. At this rate, Carol will want to go back to Exception City without having even tried farm life. Poor Dad.

"What the…" Running a hand through his brown hair, Dad breathes out pure frustration as the gates come in sight again and we haven't seen the slightest sign of a breach large enough to admit a piranha'saur, let alone a well-grown Dakotaraptor. "You *sure* about those prints, Darryl, my girl?"

I struggle to hold down a flash of anger. I mean, we can't find the thing anywhere, right? "I'm sure, Dad. Absolutely positive. You can go and look. Or—"

I grab the camera control stick, switch to the yard cam and zoom in. "There. What made those?"

Dad takes one look. "Well-grown Dakotaraptor, probably male. Sorry, Darryl. But the thing seems to be invisible."

With a sudden frown, he checks all the in-house cameras, then relaxes. No, it's not somehow in here with us, thank *God*. So where? Dad stares out the window, absently switching between the barn audios, listening to the happy stock we can see chewing their cud on the screens.

"Hey!" Harry points to the drone's screen. It's still hovering obediently near the gate, waiting for more commands.

"That was quick!" Dad peers at the truck that's just come through our inner gate. We weren't expecting any of our neighbors to get here for at least another ten minutes. "It's Riley and Sandra. Well, they can drive around and look for our invisible friend."

"If it's not on the monitors—" Harry objects.

"Then we've got a blind spot we don't know about. And by the worst luck possible, that's where the critter has parked itself."

Harry shoots me a look. I shrug. But I know what he's thinking. Dad reviews the camera coverage every year, making Harry and I walk up and down every inch of the farm, inside and out, while he checks he

8

never loses sight of us. Can we really have a blind spot? Maybe it did get out again.

But where did it get *in*?

The Wahlburgs' truck pulls into the yard, the strobe reflecting dazzlingly every time it passes over it.

"Fred's with them," Harry says, but we've all glimpsed the teenager in the back seat. No surprise. Everyone old enough to hold a gun turns out in response to a breach alarm.

Dad reaches for the Intercar mic on the console, then stiffens in horror as the Wahlburgs open the doors and start getting out. "What are they *doing?*"

I hit the button to raise the turret's windows and all three of us get our rifles up, trying to cover anywhere the uninvited guest could emerge from.

"Are you stark raving mad, Riley?" yells Dad, jerking his head upwards to the siren-light above us. "Can't you see we have a breach?"

Our neighbor puts his hands in his pockets and grins up at us. "Having yourself an exciting morning, are you, William?"

Fred can't keep a straight face and doubles over, laughing hysterically.

"All right, which one of you was it?" shouts Dad, not slow to catch on.

Riley smirks. "Fred, actually. He 'fessed up this morning, because the clunk went and damaged our drone using it to ram that raptor-foot into the ground. But really, I should have thought of it myself. Newlyweds shouldn't get away without a good—"

"I'm going to wring his neck!" Dad dives for the hatch and disappears.

"Fred, start running," Harry suggests.

Fred shrugs. "Why? It was just a prank. Everyone pranks newlyweds. Dad called Mr. Carr—and Mrs. Swayle, too—so they'd know not to rush over here when your alarm went, and they both laughed like chuckle'saurs!"

"You didn't hear what happened yesterday?" I ask grimly.

"What happened yesterday?" Sandra suddenly looks worried.

"That rex attack on the highway?"

"A family got squashed under a longneck and a truck was almost breached by raptors but got away, right?" said Riley.

"Yeah. Well, *we* were the truck." I jab my finger to the side of the house where the battered, windowless truck is parked. "And Carol was nervous enough *before* that."

The Wahlburgs move to get a view of the truck. Riley whistles, Sandra's dark skin lightens slightly, and Fred's jaw drops in the sort of excited 'wow' that just proves he wasn't in the vehicle when it sustained the damage.

"Fred!" The bellow comes from the front door. Dad's made it downstairs. "Fred, you oily gun swab, I'm going to, I'm going to..."

"Yo, Mr. Franklyn, easy now!" Fred backs away, hands raised placatingly. "I'm really sorry about the joke. I'd never have done it if I'd known you had some trouble yesterday, really I wouldn't!"

"You wouldn't have done it if you'd known we had some trouble yesterday?" roars Dad. "Really? And if we *hadn't*, you'd think that was the way to welcome a city-girl to life out-city? Seriously, you miserable hatchling?"

"Come on," says Harry, moving to the ladder. Keen to watch Fred get chewed out or hoping to help him?

I seal the windows again, sling my rifle over my shoulder and follow him. By the time we reach the front door, Carol hovers nervously in the doorway, while outside, even Riley and Sandra look shame-faced.

"We didn't know what he planned, William," Riley is saying. "I probably would have stopped him."

"I would *definitely* have stopped him." Sandra shoots Carol a sympathetic look. "I mean, what a way to welcome someone!"

11

"She was smiling hard enough when they arrived," muttered Harry.

"Yeah, but what's done is done, guess she thought she might as well enjoy the laugh." I put a hand on Carol's shoulder—she yips slightly in fright. "Oh, sorry, Carol! Are you okay? There really isn't any danger. It was just a stupid practical joke. Harry, can you…"

Harry's already moved to the House Control. The strobe-light stops flickering across the yard. Phew, that's better. Carol's shoulder is trembling under my hand.

"Come on," I tell her. "Let's go in and put the kettle on. You can meet the Wahlburgs later. They're our neighbors. Our favorite neighbors *usually*."

HARRY

Carol allows Darryl to shepherd her inside and settle her on the sofa. I go unasked to put the kettle on, eager to prove I've got more sense than Fred, even if he's a year older than me. Though let's face it, if Dad had brought home a regular tough-as-nails farmer bride, the prank would've been a good one and *we'd* all be laughing like so many chuckle'saurs right now.

Dad's stern voice rumbles on outside for a while, lecturing just Fred or his folks as well, I'm not sure. By

12

the time they troop in behind Dad, looking thoroughly deflated, the kettle's boiled and I've made a big pot of instant coffee.

Dad glances my way. "Ah, good man."

I shrug likes it's no big deal, though my spine tries to straighten a clear inch.

Darryl hurries over to pour a cup and take it straight to Carol, so I distribute mugs to our less-than-usually welcome guests.

"I, uh, I apologize for this clunk of a son of ours, Mrs. Franklyn." Fred's dad settles awkwardly on a seat opposite Carol, his fair skin darkened by more than his suntan.

"Please, call me Carol," is my new step-mom's—faint—response.

"Oh, call me Riley. Yeah, I assure you, when he came clean this morning we headed straight over to put y'all out of your misery."

No wonder they got here so fast. They were already on the way. Darryl's stern expression eases as she draws the same conclusion.

"I do appreciate *that*, Riley," mutters Dad. Apparently he's willing to forgive and forget.

"I'm Sandra," says Fred's mom, reaching across the coffee table to grip Carol's hand. "How 'bout you all come for a cook-out on Sunday?"

"Yeah, how about it?" says Riley, with painful enthusiasm.

Dad shoots a look at Carol. Sunday's only two day's time. Will she want to go outSPARK in just two days? Even to the next farm?

"I think it's our turn, isn't it? I've got some prime soft steaks in the freezer I don't want to go past their best."

"Right, you're on. We'll host you another time." Riley sips his coffee, looking relieved that everything's back to normal.

Fred catches my eye and grins sheepishly. I try to frown, but the corners of my mouth are twitching up almost against my will. Fred smirks. Great.

Fred's dad spots the smirk. As Fred reaches for a mug of coffee, Riley says, "Oh, and clunk-head here is going to do all your chores for you this morning. So's Darryl and Harry can stay in here and help their stepmom settle in. Put that down, Fred, and jump to it."

Now I'm really trying not to grin at the expression on Fred's face! Still...holding Carol's hand or...?

I finish my mugful in one big swig. "Yo, I'd better go with him. Show him what's what."

Riley frowns. "He's doing the work, remember."

Dad scowls too. "You just let him know what he needs to do, Harry, that's all."

14

"Sure, Dad, Mr. Walhburg."

I catch Fred's eye—we slip out quick, before anyone can change their mind.

JOSHUA

Even in the enclosed blackness of the 'master bedroom' I smell the city as soon as I wake. Traffic fumes and teeming humanity burn the back of my throat. I can't wait to get out of here.

I sit up and peer at the screen by the door, my head brushing the ceiling. I've finally stopped growing, just in time to save me a sore head in the morning. Yep, the main living area of the HabVi is empty of any threat, the glowing green light proclaiming it unbreached and secure.

Of course it is. I'm in-city. As though I could forget.

But I'd rather check unnecessarily now than forget when it matters.

Letting the door hiss open, I slide my body out and drop to the floor without bothering to use the footholds. Not even stopping to put the kettle on, I bend to check the computer console, scrolling down the list of contracts I bid for yesterday. Rejected, accepted, accepted, rejected... Seven accepted. Good. We can blow out of here straight after breakfast.

15

I bang on the door to the cab, which doubles as the second proper 'bedroom'. I can fit several more people in the multi-use bunks/shelves/cupboards in the living area, but Phil's my only employee at the moment. "Phil? We've got contracts. Come on, let's get moving."

No reply. Like virtually anyone I could legally employ, Phil's older than me, although not by much. Usually he respects my authority as paymaster, if nothing else. Though not so much early in the morning. I put coffee on, shove some bread, cheese, and lean 'saur slices on the fold-down table for a quick breakfast and try again.

"Phil? Come on, get *up!* D'you wanna to stay here longer than necessary?"

Stupid question. Phil doesn't like hunting all that much. He just took the job to get away from his parents' 'boring' farm. He idolizes city life, the weirdo. Well, he works for me and I'd rather be lowered into a pit of piranha'saurs—naked—than stay in-city an extra hour. "Phil, get up or skip breakfast, okay?" Silence. "Fine, skip it, but we're not stopping later when you're hungry!"

Making a coffee, I sit at the table and eat, scrolling through the contracts in more detail. Should be a nice, varied trip. Some samples, surveys, and stuff to gather, some live captures, a little culling. Nothing too complicated. The live triceratops calf will be the most challenging. On account of the live triceratops mother we're gonna have to get it away from. But the University needs one. My preference would be to find a sick mother we can put out of her misery, removing the danger and saving the calf's life. That's always a successful strategy. Dad and Uncle Z used it often.

For a moment my munching slows. I glance up at the photo-screen, where our family photos display, one after the other. There I am in a baby carrier, on Dad's front, my chubby fist waving a fresh raptor-claw. Dad's trying to get the sharp, messy thing off me, and Uncle Z's no doubt laughing his head off behind the camera. Probably he gave it to me in the first place. Dad had a lot of talks with him about 'age-appropriate toys' or so the tale went.

The picture changes—now I'm about eight, and we're all posing in front of the new 'Vi. Three shades of brown skin, near-black hair, and brown eyes. Race indeterminate. I don't know my family tree on my mother's side, but Dad's and Uncle Z's family tree is enough to explain that by itself! Hispanic, African, European, Native American, it's all up there.

My eyes move from Dad to Uncle Z. Maybe one day our little family will be together again, somehow. If only we...

No. Firmly, I start chewing again. Right now, I'm on my own, and I need to get on with life. Though I may just drop dead if I have to stay in-city much longer. I swallow my last bite and get to my feet, stow everything quickly away and move to the cab door.

"Right, Phil, we're leaving. So I'm coming in. Hope you're decent." I hit the "open" button and the door slides back. I duck into the space, settle in the driver's seat and look to the side. What the...?

No sleeping bag. No personal stuff of any kind. Just a half page of scrawl lying on the seat-bed. I snatch it up.

Hi Josh,

Got offered a real city job, have to start this morning. Sure you understand.

Phil

I stare at it, then read it again. Anger fills me so full I can't speak.

"Understand?" The yell rips from me at last. "*Understand?* We've got seven contracts to fulfill, you good for nothing...! You knew I'd placed the bids yesterday, you swine! *Understand?* Like heck I understand!"

Crumpling the note, I throw it on the floor, which goes absolutely nowhere in relieving my feelings. A tight ball of anxiety swiftly replaces the fury in my chest. Now I can't leave until I've replaced Mr. Real City Job. Unbelievable!

I could swear Dad's lucky mascot—a statue of Saint Desmond on the dashboard—is trying to catch my eye, so I breathe deeply for several minutes, forcing myself to calm down and making a mental note to pay my employee on departure from the city in future, not on arrival, never mind what's normal. Phil's left me totally in the lurch.

The city smell clogs my nose, making me want to gag. The tall buildings tower overhead, seeming to bend in, blocking the sky, threatening to topple on me. We should be driving out of here right now.

Gah! I go back into the living area, sit at the console and start drafting an advertisement for the jobs site.

Wanted: Hunter's assistant. With experience or willing to learn. To start immediately.

Normally I'd add the standard line: *Job unsuitable for claustrophobes or those of a nervous disposition*, but I don't bother.

Anyone. Quickly.

19

HARRY

The chores are done—I didn't help Fred *much*—and we're back in the farmyard. Has Carol calmed down yet? She still looked so delicately tearful when we came out. All, 'I'm *together*, but look how much effort it's costing me'.

Fred grabs my arm, towing me around to the side of the house. "Yo, come on, show me the truck!"

My eyes fall on the mangled vehicle and for a moment I see that old Dakotaraptor matriarch, teeth and leathery face and big orange-blue ruff feathers, ripping the grille from my window; I feel the tire iron in my clenched fist as my adrenalin-flooded brain calculates whether to strike for the nose or the eye, knowing that with nowhere to run, neither will help...

I blink, shake my head slightly, and the memory evaporates. I'm not too anxious to go back in the house, so I follow Fred as he moves around the truck, examining it excitedly.

"Wow!" He fits his fingers into the claw marks in Dad's door. "They really tried to peel you out of there, didn't they?"

"Yo, that's nothing!" I take the grille by my window, which is hanging in position in a deceptively innocent way, and lift it to the side, then poke Carol's to display the gap.

Fred's eyes bulge and he whistles. "*Outage!* How'd you even survive?"

"Well, Carol had just got clawed, and the pack matriarch was literally about to shove her head in and get bashed by my tire iron when the HabVi got a clear shot at last and ran them off."

"A tire iron, Harry? Seriously? Where was your rifle? What HabVi? How bad was Carol hurt? How did you get in that mess, anyway?"

I roll my eyes at this barrage of questions and pluck a handful of blue-orange ruff feathers from my grille. This story could take a while. Hopping up, I plunk myself on the scratched hood, avoiding the pool of dried raptor blood. Fred isn't so picky or doesn't realize what it is, anyway, he sits right on it.

"Well, it was a completely uneventful run from Exception, right up until..."

DARRYL

Riley and Sandra seem to sense this is not the day to overstay their welcome. When Dad checks the cameras and finds that Harry and Fred are now goofing off by the truck, chores obviously complete, the Wahlburgs are on their feet at once, politely taking their leave. Fred is ordered into their truck by his dad, with dire warnings that he will fix the drone when he gets home or the cost is coming out of his allowance. And off they go.

"Oh, honey." Dad promptly wraps Carol in his arms. "I am *so* sorry about our stupid neighbors. Pranks are customary when people marry, you see, and that kid's too much of a clunk to realize that you wouldn't be expecting it. Heck, it never crossed my mind anyone would be so inconsiderate! Never crossed my mind at *all.*"

"Or mine," I mutter, picturing us up there in the turret, racking our brains over the mysterious footprints. If it wasn't for Carol, I'd be tempted to smile. But she still looks so shaky.

"Right, chores are done, it's time for breakfast." Dad leads Carol back inside and Harry follows eagerly.

Just another day on the farm, after all.

JOSHUA

I can smell alcohol on the man's breath before he's even entered the vehicle. And he's the last applicant. Out of a grand total of three, though I waited two days for replies. Just great. But Dad's told me often enough that rudeness never helped anyone and harmed many, so I shake his hand—pretending I can't feel the tremor—and wave him to a seat at the fold-down table to the side of the HabVi's main living area.

I focus on the drunk sitting across the table from me and start my pointless list of questions.

"You got any experience with hunting?"

Zip.

"Know how to load a gun?"

Of course.

"Load this one, please."

Um...

"Why do you want to become a hunter?"

Feel like a change.

"Have you got quick reactions and good senses?"

Good as the day I was born.

"Any history of problems with alcohol?"

Never touched a drop in my life.

I leave it there. An honest alcoholic might be better than no one at all—that precious extra pair of eyes—but a lying alcoholic I'm not taking for even one trip. *A liar is always more trouble than he's worth.* Another of Dad's sayings.

"Thank you for your time, but you're not quite what I'm looking for."

I show him out the large side door, then retreat from the noise and stink of the city and sling myself back into my chair. Have I done the right thing? I have to head out again; I've got those contracts to fulfill. But the first man was so ancient I'd have been caring for him half the time, the second barely able to defer to me for the length of the interview and the alcoholic…a liar.

Maybe I should've taken the old man. Any pair of eyes would be better than…but no, when I performed my discreet eye test (by appearing to accidentally open the door to the fully enclosed pen at the back of the vehicle which before each interview I always ensure displays 'OCCUPIED – live velociraptor – for delivery Exception Central Zoo') not even the briefest, tiniest flicker of concern crossed his face, sure proof he couldn't make out the words on the display. Eyes that couldn't see would only give a fatally false sense of security.

So what about the guy who didn't want to be working for a teenager? Eighteen's still technically a teenager, right? That's what the guy's attitude screamed, anyway.

Or the liar?

How to choose? Well, I sent them all away, so I'll just have to fulfill these few contracts solo, then I can come back and try again.

If you're still alive, whispers a pessimistic voice in my head.

It will only take a couple of weeks, I think back. *They're easy contracts, very little outdoor work. I'll make out okay.*

Pessimistic Voice slips in the last word. *You hope.*

Enough. You're born, you live, you die. That's nature. I know I shouldn't go off on my own, but I can't stay in-city another moment. I feel like I'm suffocating. I press the button to retract my stabilizers, seal all the doors, make a quick circuit of the living area, stowing *stuff*, and in minutes I'm in the driver's seat and pulling away.

Once the city fence falls behind and the horizon opens out before me, I can breathe again. Dad would shake his head at me, if he knew.

But I'd rather die happy than stay in *there*.

HARRY

My chores are almost done and my stomach's rumbling. I'm looking forward to the cook-out at lunchtime, but hopefully breakfast will be ready when I get back to the house. Carol turns out to be a good cook, if a little too fancy and healthy. She took charge of the kitchen on the first day, straight after breakfast. She calmed right down once she was rummaging through cupboards and inspecting the contents of the freezer. "I may not," she declared, "be able to look after all those—" a delicate shudder— "*creatures*, but this I can do!"

Darryl and Dad yielded the cooking to her happily enough. Dad's cooking has never exactly been great, and Daryl would rather be worming edmo calves than in the kitchen, any day. I'm already getting used to the tasty meals.

Carol liked the new computer console Dad got for her, too, and seems happy with the faster Net connection. She spends quite a few hours a day in the spare bedroom—Carol's office, as it now is—doing her fashion designs. And she is nice. A bit wimpy and worried about her looks and jaw-droppingly ignorant about farm stuff, but…nice. I guess things aren't going too badly, despite that awful start.

A chime issues from my ScreamerBand. Someone's at the gate, a stranger without a pass code. Fred and his folks aren't due until lunch. Well, Dad will decide whether to let them in. I return the pitchfork to the straw stack and tap the Barn Control to open the doors, letting the cows out onto the pasture. In the distance, a familiar HabVi cruises up the drive. The hunters!

I dash around the barn, checking all's well, then race to the yard, where the huge vehicle now stands. The third hunter is dropping easily from the cab, Dad and Darryl are there greeting them and everyone is smiling, though Carol, hovering in the farmhouse doorway, looks a bit nervous. Hunters have a reputation in-city, don't they? For being, what do they call it, *rough*?

Or maybe it's the three fresh raptor heads decorating spikes on the front of the HabVi's roof. I peer more closely at the one on the left...blue-orange ruff feathers. That old matriarch won't be trying to eat any more thirteen-year-old farm boys.

"Recognize anyone?" grins the hunter who just got down from the cab. His white teeth blaze against his skin, even darker than Sandra's, and they've dressed up for the visit by putting on their claw necklaces. If only I'd thrown mine on this morning. A stab of envy pricks me as I see that Darryl and Dad have both had time to grab theirs.

"Yeah, that old..." I glance at Dad and swallow the next word, "that old one's nose nearly had a date with my tire iron."

The hunter snorts and shakes his head. "Think that would have helped, do you?"

"Well, I wouldn't have died like a squealing piglet!"

The hunter grins, and one of the other two claps me on the shoulders. "The boy's right, West. That's a big help to any man." He glances at Darryl. "Or woman. You the gal who was shooting so straight, right?"

Darryl turns pink. "Yeah..."

Hunter number two—Hispanic-looking—reaches up into the cab and takes something down, holds it out to Darryl. "These are yours, then."

Darryl accepts the neat pair of raptor claws, looking pleased. "That the clean kill I left on the highway, right?"

The hunter nods, then shoots an approving glance at her necklace. "You can add them to your box."

Argh, I want my necklace on! Darryl's modest-looking one has only three claws, a big one and a fine matched pair, but anyone who matters knows an odd number means she's got more than she can string on one necklace. My necklace is still evens—I've got five pairs, but if I get one more pair, I can cut mine down to three too, without it looking like I'm claiming more credit than's due me. But five-pair isn't bad, at my age. Fred's only got three-pair, and Bentley Carr only moved to odds a few months ago, and he's fifteen. Maybe I can slip and get it, if we all go inside.

Thiago is the name of the second hunter, and fair-skinned, blue-eyed Ed is the third.

"We're about to have breakfast," Dad says. "Come join us." He shoots Carol a quick look. "Can we rustle up enough, honey? We can just get some bread and cheese out."

Carol stops looking nervous at once and goes into efficient-mode. "Don't worry, it will be *fine*, darling." She disappears into the kitchen.

The hunters' eyes follow her admiringly. "That is one elegant farm lady you've got there, sah," says Thiago.

Dad is trying not to look too pleased. "No farm lady. Carol's from the city. We're just married. We were bringing her home when we got into that heap of trouble the other day."

West looks sympathetic, the other two roar with laughter.

"Of all the luck!"

"Bad luck, man!"

Dad grins ruefully and leads them into the house.

DARRYL

When a massive quantity of Carol's good cooking has been devoured and many stories have been told — tall tales and true ones all mixed up together until Carol looks cross-eyed — and Harry's snuck off and come back with his necklace resting on his puffed-out chest and been duly congratulated by the hunters, and Dad's signed as a witness on the cull report that will allow the hunters to claim bounty on the raptors, we all, inevitably, head back out to the HabVi to inspect the hunters' wares. No one's implying that they wouldn't have helped us for free, but buying something is a polite way of giving them a more tangible thank you.

"What have you got in the way of exotic hides?" Dad asks, after examining various claws, teeth, and common hides, none of which we really need. And after two recent trips in-city there's not much in the way of useful bits and pieces they can sell us either— many HabVis carry a small stock of such items. "Anything really spectacular? Carol is a fashion designer, you know." He looks at Carol. "Maybe they've got something you'd like; you know, something really inspiring."

Carol frowns doubtfully. From what I've seen, in-city fashions in most things tend to ignore the reason for those big city fences as much as possible.

West exchanges grins with the other two, his teeth gleaming again, and climbs into the HabVi.

"Wait till you see this," says Thiago.

They seem so smug that when West comes back out holding a large flat box I can't help crowding forward eagerly with Harry. West gives the box to Ed to hold, removes the lid, and lifts out a glistening piece of leather, roughly the size and shape of a triceratops' frill, but patterned in vibrant yellow, blue, and red.

I touch it carefully. "Wow, that's soft!"

"What is it?" asks Harry.

Dad takes the hanging part and spreads it out, inspecting the shape. "It's a frill, right? But I haven't seen any 'saur round here with a frill like that. Where d'you get it?"

West nods. "Frill, yeah. We didn't hunt it ourselves, we traded for it, with some guys from far up north. They've got these things—dilophosaurs—up in the forests there. Very dangerous, very stealthy—spit poison, just to compound it all."

I've heard of those poison-spitting killers. Worse than raptors, in some ways. "How do you hunt them in a forest?" I stare at the beautiful frill. "Do you have to do it on *foot?*"

"Nah, it wouldn't be you doing the hunting. They've got some special little forest rigs, all enclosed with shooting slits, that fit between the trees. Still dangerous, though. If the rig gets tipped over, you're finished. But the things are such a menace there's almost no restrictions on hunting them, and the frills are worth a lot when properly cured, so there's always someone game to try. Can't say I'd fancy it myself; I'm used to open country."

Carol stares at the piece of leather, a strange distant look on her face.

"What do you think, honey?" asks Dad hopefully. "D'you like it?"

Carol blinks, then reaches out—gingerly—to touch it at last. "Oh! It *is* soft!" Her gaze grows less focused again. "It will be the grand collar on a lady's…no, a *man's* cape—a cape of thick black leather—the *lady's* cape will have a feather ruff, like…" she shudders, but her eyes are alight, "like those nightmares had around their faces."

The hunters look blank in the face of this and Harry grins, so I translate, "Raptor feathers. D'you have any colorful raptor ruff feathers?"

"Oh. Yeah. We've got plenty of those. Some quite fine ones."

"They need to be glorious ones!" Carol strokes the frill contemplatively. "Yes, the two capes will be the centerpieces of my autumn collection! Daring, original, *wild!* It will take the catwalk by storm!"

"Wow, it sounds amazing, honey." A couple of bags of the best raptor feathers are taken into the house for Carol to look through out of the wind, while Dad starts haggling over the frill—though not as hard as he would if the hunters hadn't saved all our lives three days ago.

HARRY

Carol's now selecting a rich golden steg hide for her lady's cape and inspecting several other fine leathers. She's very picky, but then, her designer-wear is supposed to be top notch or so Dad's told us several times. I'm glad she's found something about 'saurs to get her enthusiastic, but it's pretty boring. Darryl hovers attentively but a glazed look is creeping into her eyes.

As though reading my mind, Ed catches my eye and jerks his head to the 'Vi. "Want to look inside?"

"Yeah!" The childishly enthusiastic response spills out before I can check it, but he just grins and waves me ahead of him, patiently spending half an hour showing off the different equipment and features. It's not a new vehicle, but far from the biggest scrap-heap trundling around out there. New enough to have the standard rear pen design and dual "bedrooms" above and in the main cab area.

West owns half of it—I thought he seemed like the boss—the other two own a quarter each. HabVis cost so much, it's a common arrangement, though it sure as anything forces them to learn to get along with each other. Ed seems to have drawn the short straw, in that he sleeps in the top cupboard bunk in the living area, much smaller and more cramped than either of the others.

"What's in here?" I point at the red light glowing on one of the critter cages.

"Baby anchylosaurid."

33

"An armadillion? Really? Can I see?"

He opens the cage and lets me take out the heavy bundle of armored scales, about the size of a large cat. I keep a precautionary hand around the tail, with that nasty spiked ball on the end, but the armadillion just snuffles my hand curiously. "Wow, he's tame!"

"Yeah, name's Terence. We had him literally out of the egg, from a nest that got trampled in a rex stampede, a month ago. We let him run around the living area most of the time. We kinda like him, to be honest. He'll have to go to a new home when he gets bigger, but we'll make sure it's a good one."

"Can I show him to Ryl? She'd love him!"

"Sure. He won't run away."

I climb down carefully with the heavy baby, all the same. "Look, Ryl!"

Darryl, still busy being a supportive step-daughter and quite obviously—at least to me—showing more interest in the exact shade and texture of the leather than she really feels, has stayed with Carol all this time, though I'm sure she'd have rather looked around the 'Vi. The baby armadillion is more than she can resist, though, and she has him off me at once.

"Terence," I tell her. "They saved him from a trampled nest. Going to need a new home sometime, as well." I eye Dad. "Dad?"

"Hmm?"

"Can we have Terence?"

"What?" His eye falls on Darryl's armful. "No!"

"Why not? He's really tame."

"Yeah, and he's going to get *really* big. Give it six months and with one tantrum he'll destroy half the house or put someone in the hospital. And he'd have to live outside once he was half-grown, anyway. Smashing fences, knocking holes in barns. Like having a tank around, but a tank with a mind of its own—a pea-sized mind, even worse. No."

"But he's going to need a good home when he's bigger—"

"Yeah, a *good* home. An armadillion-proof home. Not a farm. You did well the other day, both of you, and if you want a little treat I'll get you one. But you're *not* having a baby armadillion."

"Huh." But I recognize a lost cause and simply stroke Terence apologetically. "Sorry Terence, you're going to end up in a zoo."

"Come on, Harry, he's cute, but it's the best place for him," says Darryl.

"Ugh, you're so grown up and sensible these days," I complain. "Considering you never got to have a proper pet, I'd have thought you'd be all for it."

"No, I just don't want to be mending things and mending things and mending things and…"

"Yeah, like I said, sensible!"

35

"Have you got a piranha'saur?" Darryl asks Ed.

I stiffen hopefully.

"Sorry, none at the moment."

"Typical," I mutter. I've had three different piranha'saurs since I was seven, but Darryl's evil cat killed them all. Most annoying was when that one got through our fence and Dad sold it to Fred because I'd already got one, and the very next week the cat killed mine. Now that rat-slaughtering hairball has finally died of old age, Dad wants to buy me something and there isn't one to buy. I suppose I'm too old for piranha'saurs, really. But it would've been nice to have just one that died of old age.

Darryl looks so quietly relieved I appreciate that she asked. Yeah, someone *else's* piranha'saur can be a pain to live with. As in, a pain in the fingers—and sometimes the ankles.

Hmm. I couldn't have one now, could I? Carol would shriek every time she saw it, let alone if it actually nipped her.

DARRYL

Terence is awfully cute, there's no getting around that. Even Carol peers cautiously at his baby face—from a distance—and smiles. Then her eyes wander over his back in a more thoughtful manner.

36

"I doubt you could do much with armadillion scales," I tell her. "They're very thick and the hide is incredibly thick, too. And they won't sell you Terence for *that*."

Carol's eyes widen, and she hastens to assure everyone that she had no thought of incorporating *Terence himself* into her collection. "He's far too sweet, in a bony sort of way. And you're right, that sort of ridged scale would be hard to use." She turns to West again. "Okay, I'd like those three hides and the bones and the feathers. Those teeth and that selection of claws."

We've probably got some of this stuff around the farm already, but Dad says nothing. Lives saved and all that. The three hunters, from their happy expressions, are beginning to feel well thanked.

When Dad moves to pay for the second lot of stuff, Carol waves him away. "Oh, no, dear. The frill was your little gift and I *love* it, but I must pay for all these other things from my business account. I always choose the raw materials in person. When the designs are done, I'll ship them to the tailors. But I need them here for inspiration. So I can *see* it." She's getting a little distant again, but soon returns to the farmyard and takes care of the transaction. Despite her clear creative streak, I've already noticed her business-like efficiency. I guess the combination is why she's successful.

A peep from my ScreamerBand says that someone with a pass code has just come through the gates. Harry turns to look up the drive, and I look too.

The Wahlburgs.

"Heh, and I haven't even got the grill going yet," mutters Dad. He glances at the hunters. "We're having a cook-out and you guys are very welcome to stay— hope you will—but I must go and get things started."

He heads into the house. Carol follows, carrying some of her purchases, with Thiago bringing the rest. I should probably go and help. Terence is starting to wriggle, anyway, and he's getting awfully heavy. "Where shall I put Terence?" I ask West.

"Oh, pop him down on the ground once that truck is stopped. Let him wander around. He's really slow, he can't go far. He can't resist a piece of apple, anyway. Wave one around and he'll be charging back for it at a whole one mile per hour."

I wait until Riley and Sandra and Fred are all out of the vehicle and the doors closed, before putting the restless baby down—a little nervously. One thing Dad didn't mention, and I'm not sure Harry realizes, is that a really large, hard to handle breed like an armadillion, tamed right from hatching, is actually worth quite a lot of money. More than Dad would want to pay, even leaving aside the practical issues. No way they'd sell him to us, for pet prices. So I don't want any harm to befall the valuable little critter in our yard.

Terence toddles slowly off, nibbling at tufts of grass and sniffing at clods of mud and the hunters remain unconcerned, so I give up worrying about it.

JOSHUA

No birds are singing when I open my eyes. It's midday. A yawn stretches my jaws wide open. I stayed up all night doing that nocturnal survey for the Mammalian Protection Institute, one contract I could get ticked off at once. Well, I've no need to get up. It's not like I have to set a good example to my employees or anything, is it? Huh, I wish.

I turn over and snuggle into my sleeping bag—Dad's old sleeping bag—drawing it cozily up around my neck although there isn't really any chill. No, there's really no...*yawn*...no rush...

...I fix the meat carefully onto the spiderline, watching Dad checking the contents of his little rex-nesting backpack. "Can't I do it? I'm fourteen now."

Dad doesn't look up. "No."

"I've done several rex nests already. Don't I need the practice?"

Dad shakes his head, fastening the pack's silent-release buckles—no Velcro, no zips, no clanking bits of metal. "Not

39

this nest, Josh. You're not doing this nest, not while your Uncle Z or I are around to do it. Well, not 'til we're too arthritic to move quiet, anyway."

"But I can run faster than you even now!"

Dad rests his hand on my shoulder for a moment. "Seriously, Josh? No one outruns a rex, you know that. Speed is not the issue here. Just experience."

"Yeah, and how will I gain that if you won't let me get any?"

"Not this nest, Josh. It's the darndest nest in the whole—"

"So much for 'You're a man when you can control yourself and think through the consequences of your actions, never mind what the silly law says.'" I sound sulky, but I can't help it. Dad says one minute that I'm a man and the next he treats me like a child again.

The sulk in my voice earns me a scathing look. "Yeah? I stand by that, but I'm not seeing it right now."

So as not to prove his point, I swallow the next whine that rises to my lips and ask instead, "Is it really so dangerous?"

Dad shrugs. "Do you have to ask? The nest is way up there in the crags, no possibility of cover, of course it's risky. Okay, we've staked out this area since yesterday evening, monitoring for carni'saurs, and we've done this nest many times before so we know the terrain, and the odds are well in our favor. But yeah, it's more dangerous than most rex nests, not that any of these contracts are the safest money."

"Why take it then?" I can't help muttering. I kind of want to do it myself, to…to prove myself, but if I can't, if it really is too dangerous, I'd rather we didn't do it at all.

Dad laughs, and a snort drifts down through the turret hatch from where Uncle Z is continuing to monitor the 'saur activity.

"No one goes rex-nesting just for the money, Josh. You know that."

Ain't that the truth. Creeping up to the nest of the largest land predator ever to walk the earth and sterilizing its eggs isn't something any sane person would do merely for hard cash. But it's an important job. Important for people's safety. SPARKed people, that is. Really important for farms. If someone doesn't do this, farm folks pay for it.

The only two carni'saurs large enough to threaten a modern electric fence are T. rex and spinosaurs, but an out-of-control rex, especially, can cause a total breach of a small farm fence and considerable damage even to a city fence, so the Dinosaur Activity and Population department (or DAPdep, as most people call them) control their numbers closely. Since juvenile rex are by far the biggest offenders when it comes to blundering into fences the goal is to ensure that each area has a stable population of nice mature rex — which will stay away from electricity — just sufficient to keep

41

the herbi'saurs in balance, with only enough chicks hatched out to replace them.

Sterilizing the eggs (as opposed to culling the chicks) has the added bonus of tying up the mother rex for three months at a time, to say nothing of being—usually—the less risky option. And after guarding apparently undamaged eggs for three months with almost no food, she'll need to recuperate and most likely won't seek to mate again until the following year.

"But this *nest, wouldn't it be easier to cull the chicks once they're hatched out?" I can't help asking.*

"Ever tried to cull a T. rex's chicks without shooting the mother first?" demands Uncle Z, from up above me.

Which is illegal, of course, unless your life is in danger, and you'd better be able to prove that *to DAPdep.*

"Hey, you *keep your eyes on those screens, big bro," says Dad, drawing another snort from Uncle Z, who probably hadn't taken his eyes off them in the first place. They've both been hunting since Dad was a few years younger than me, when they stowed away in a hunter's 'Vi to escape their father's farm—and his beatings. My Grandpa wasn't a well man, that's what Dad says. Uncle Z's less forgiving.*

Apart from the fact that shooting the mother rex wouldn't go down good with DAPdep, I've seen what an angry rex can do to the fragile safety of a HabVi. Four wet behind the ears city boys, that was. Very much was. *I*

42

shudder. No, we don't want a rex tearing apart Dad's and Uncle Z's pride and joy and gobbling us up. Dad's right. The nest, however chancy, is a safer target.

"Right, I'm set." Dad shrugs his rucksack on and steps to the side door. No gun to tap against rocks and give him away. Just his pack, communicators, his wits—and all that experience.

I climb back up to the turret, meat in one hand, and push the button to recall the drone, currently maintaining altitude overhead, lending its cameras and infrared to Uncle Z's efforts. Opening the under-hatch of the drone dome, I hook the end of the spiderline onto the drone—not that the material has anything to do with spiders but they call it that 'cause it's as strong as spider silk—balance the meat on the hatch and shut it quick, before the meat can slither out. I'll have to rinse it with odor neutralizer later to get rid of any traces of meat juices.

Wiping my hands on an odor wipe and pulling one of the swivel seats into position, I settle into it and take hold of the drone controls properly. "Okay, Dad." I speak softly, to double-check my own throat mic is working properly.

"Right, wait for my mark. And you, bro, keep your eyes peeled." Dad's voice comes only through my earpiece, so he's re-testing his mic too.

Uncle Z just snorts again. "Little bro, get a move on before something does wander along and we've done all this stake-out for nothing."

43

"I'm gone, I'm gone."

I hear the door slide open and a moment later I see Dad jogging up the hillside. We've parked as far up as we can, so there's only a short stretch of steepening grass before the rocks begin.

He's soon out of sight.

HARRY

"Yo, that's the one I was going to bash on the nose," I tell Fred, pointing up to the left-hand head. I display the handful of feathers I pulled from the truck grille two days ago and had forgotten in my pocket until now.

"Big b...uh...brute," says Fred, glancing at his dad.

"Looks like you guys have been hard at work," says Riley to West and Ed. Thiago hasn't come back from playing porter for Carol yet.

They shrug. "We put down one wounded raptor right there on the road," says West. "Only left two healthy pack members and with their matriarch wounded they weren't that difficult to track."

"Well, a good job, anyway." Sandra gives them an approving look. No one likes raptors around once they've got a taste for car-jacking—desperate wounded ones even less so. "Do you have any kitchen spices?"

44

"We've only got salt, pepper, and garlic powder in quantities to sell."

"I'll take some garlic powder."

By the time the food is ready Carol's slipped into something casually elegant and is standing handing out plates and making sparkly, sophisticated conversation that's leaving most of the adults—and Fred—a bit dazzled. I guess I'm getting used to her, 'cause I'm not so tongue-tied now. She's clearly enjoying the impromptu party, even if it's just a cook-out. Once the steaks are served, she and Sandra really get talking.

"Good," mutters Darryl, slipping a piece of apple to Terence, who's made his way around to the patio to join us.

"Good what?"

"Hopefully that raptor foot hasn't torpedoed her easiest female friendship, good."

I glance at Carol and Sandra again. "Oh, right. Hey, Terence isn't that dumb. He found us."

Darryl looks faintly guilty. "Nah, he found the apple. West told me it's his favorite."

"Oh." Shame. It would be nice to think the critter was brighter than a pea, though I know it's unlikely. "Oh well."

"Hey, is that yours?" Fred's finally noticed Terence.

"Nah, he belongs to the hunters. He's really tame, though."

Another peep from my ScreamerBand. Someone else with a code. Who is it now?

"Sounds like Father Ben's van," says Darryl, as the vehicle pulls up round the other side of the house. "I thought he was saying Mass over on the far side of the county today?"

But the figure that swings around the side of the house is indeed tall and familiar, darker skinned than Sandra but not as dark as West, dressed all in black from his Stetson to his sturdy boots and calling, "I hope you saved some for me!"

"There's plenty, come and join us." Dad hurries to fill a plate. "But what are you doing here today?"

"The Maxwell's children have come down with chicken pox," says Father Benedict, accepting the plate and taking a seat, loosening his clerical collar slightly. "Well, I can't risk spreading that around every house I visit, so I've come to say Mass for the newlyweds instead. The Maxwells can have your next Sunday. But I seem to be gate-crashing a party."

"Nah," says Dad. "Riley and Sandra were coming around anyway, and this here's West, Thiago, and Ed, who helped us out of a heap of trouble a few days ago and just dropped in to say hi. You're very welcome and so's Mass."

I'm a bit torn now between playing with Terence, talking to the super-cool hunters some more, or chatting to Father Benedict, who's slightly younger than Dad and a whole lot of fun. But the hunters are soon engrossed with Dad again, talking shop, and Father Benedict joins Darryl, Fred, and me around Terence.

"What are you going to do with that when it grows up, Harry?"

"It belongs to the hunters," I repeat.

"Glad to hear it. Nice little fellow, though. Oh, thanks, Darryl." My sis has just given him a slice of apple for Terence but, eyes twinkling, he takes a bite of it himself, making us all laugh. Terence stretches his tiny head up, eyes searching for the source of the smell.

Father Benedict smiles and relents. "Okay, okay, little guy. Here you go." As soon as Terence has chomped down the apple, he looks from Darryl to me. "So, kids, what happened to your truck?"

He speaks lightly, but a worried look lurks in his eye. Dad's been too busy with Carol to do more than pull the vehicle under the lean-to in case of a rainstorm—he's got his farm truck for daily use and the hunting truck for a spare—but Father Benedict clearly got a good look as he walked past.

"Oh, that," I say.

Father Benedict raises an eyebrow. "It didn't look like 'oh, that' to me."

"It was *awesome!*" says Fred.

"Without even having heard the story yet I still feel able to say with perfect confidence, *Fred, you're a clunkhead.*"

Darryl and I burst out laughing. Yep, Father Ben knows Fred!

JOSHUA

Dad's moving fast, because soon I glimpse him again, higher up the slope, a flicker of green camo jacket moving between two outcrops.

"Okay, Josh." His voice speaks in my ear again. "Put the drone up, start to lure the she-rex away. I'm going silent now."

"Understood." I speak very softly, just in case that mother rex has her ears really wide open. "Going silent" means I shouldn't speak to him again, not unless something's happening Dad needs to know about.

I have the drone re-deployed in moments, its props straining under the weight of that big—well, big for our drone—chunk of meat. It's barely a mouthful for a full-grown rex, but after a month's egg-guarding the she-rex will salivate at the mere whiff of it. And be prepared to leave her nest for a few minutes to grab it.

That's the plan, anyway.

Uncle Z *ignores me, moving steadily back and forth around the turret, scanning those screens, looking out through the windows. Without the drone's height—and heat sensors—he's partially blind, so I need to hurry up.*

There. *There's the nest and the she-rex, a well-grown, fairly brownish creature with a bushy red-orange crest. Already lifting her head, nostrils the size of my clenched fists flaring at the scent of the meat. She circles her nest checking all's well, then once again turns her huge head towards that tempting smell, crest feathers rising hopefully.*

I keep the drone at a decent altitude. If I misjudge it and she grabs the meat at once we'll have to start all over again.

Come on. *I manage not to mutter it out loud.* Come on...

She takes a step away from the nest. Then another.

That's right. This way...

I lead her down the narrow gully by which she enters and leaves her nest site, towards the place I've picked out. Just far enough away to allow a quiet, experienced hunter to work on the eggs unheard, but not so far away that the she-rex is likely to panic and return to her eggs before she's got the tidbit.

Lumbering into a trot, she snatches at the meat, but it's just too high. Here we are. *I move the drone up over the side of the rocky slope and catch the meat in the narrow gap between two rocks. A quick tug with the drone, and the* spiderline pulls free of the meat, leaving it wedged neatly in place. It will take the rex time to maneuver up that slope without overbalancing and even longer to get her head into the right position to actually seize the meat. But it's not impossible, so she's unlikely to give up until she's got it.

I raise one hand in a thumbs up to Uncle Z and whisk the drone up to high altitude, hearing his slight breath of relief as the heat sensors come back into play and his field of vision increases. I keep one mobile drone camera directed at the rex, now cautiously edging up the slope, trying not to let her huge head overbalance her, and focus the other down into the nest hollow.

There's Dad, already crouched beside the mound, his backpack open, leaning over the nearest egg as he injects the sterilization fluid into it. Deftly, he withdraws the syringe and slides the needle into the next egg, pushing the plunger down another five mil. And again. Three eggs. About normal.

The syringe cap on, he slips it back into his pack, pulls out the odor neutralizer and sprays the nest quickly. Rex don't usually abandon a nest due to human scent, but it depends what experiences this she-rex has had.

Moments later, he's got the backpack fastened and he's inching his way silently up the rocky slope.

But the rex has just seized the meat. Darn, she's smart, this one. Should've taken her much longer to figure out how to get it. Smart or lucky.

"Rex on her way back," I murmur, very softly.

Maybe I'm imagining the flash of tension that goes through Dad's shoulders, but he keeps moving, slow and painstaking. If he knocks two rocks together, the she-rex will be back into that hollow like a juggernaut of motherly wrath with a mouthful of ten-inch teeth.

Not that she's moving all that slowly as it is, lumbering along at a brisk walk, happy with her unexpected snack and keen to get back on duty. Gah!

I drop the drone again, trying to tickle the rex's head with the hanging spiderline, but she shakes her head as though dismissing a mosquito and tramps on. Dad's only ten feet from the rim of the hollow. Hurry, hurry! *At least he's high enough she can't step on him by accident.*

Argh, no! *Too late...*

"Dad, freeze!"

DARRYL

When everyone's finished eating and the conversation starts to dwindle I pop into the house with Dad to get things ready for Mass. First, though, we put a second chair into the spare...into Carol's office and close the shutters for privacy.

"Confessional's ready when you are, Father," Dad calls out the kitchen window.

51

After a little discussion among themselves, the hunters asked to stay for Mass—Thiago, at least, is clearly Catholic. They're very welcome, of course. Usually there would be several other families here, but Father Benedict has failed to round up any of them at such short notice. Gone visiting friends and relatives. Since we don't really have any relatives, we don't tend to visit so far afield on a Sunday. Mostly we hang out with the Walhburgs, the Swayles, and the Carrs, our closest neighbors.

The Swayles and Carrs are Evangelicals and Nothing In Particular, respectively. They both come to our Carol Service, which we alternate with the Wahlburgs and one of the other Catholic families, and the Swayles come to our Pentecost All-night Power Vigil, but other than that we only mix for work and social. Social mostly with the Wahlburgs and Carrs, since Maurice Carr, Riley, and Dad all grew up together, while Tina Swayle is a lot younger than them.

Father Benedict heads into the confessional with Thiago while Dad and I move the sofas to the side of the lounge and add folding seats until there's a place for everyone. Dad fetches the key and puts it in the door in the wall, behind which is a tiny alcove-sized room housing the family's tabernacle. Putting it in a separate room, however small, means that we can use the living room normally most of the time, though we tend to cross ourselves when we walk right past the door.

"Thank you, Father." Thiago finally emerges, looking cheerful despite—or because of—his long stint with Father Benedict. "I'm glad we happened to be here today. In our line of work, it's good to keep on top of these things."

I pop in next. It's mostly minor stuff, like a few bad thoughts about Carol and getting cross with Harry, but I can't help adding, "I only really thought about it the next day, Father, but when I thought those raptors were going to eat us—I mean, I really did think that was how it was probably going to end—I wasn't thinking about God at all. I mean, I didn't really have *time*, I was so busy trying to fend the things off and keep us alive, but...I don't know, that still bothers me a little bit."

Father Benedict thinks about that for so long I start to get nervous. I thought I was mostly asking for advice with that one, but maybe it was, like, a *really bad sin*.

"That's a difficult one," he says at last, his tone merely contemplative. I breathe a little easier. "No question lifting your mind to your maker is best when in danger of death, but if doing so is going to *ensure* your death, when your death is not otherwise certain, it almost counts as, if not outright suicidal, certainly as being *careless* with your life. I'm inclined to encourage you to think more about your prayer life from day-to-day, but not to agonize about your omission. I think it *was* an omission, but if you are closer to Him in your general living, it will be easier for you to lift up your heart in such a situation without being dangerously distracted. Does that make sense?"

"Yes, Father."

Fred goes in next and comes out red in the face and biting his lip. I guess Father Benedict just used a fairly dull blade to cut through Fred's self-absorption and make him think about the sort of welcome he gave Carol. Fred avoids my eyes and slinks off to do his penance somewhere else.

By the time everyone's been through except Carol and Ed—West's Catholic too; at any rate, he stamped his way into the confessional muttering and grumbling after a shove from Thiago—our dining room table has been moved to the lounge, Father Benedict's portable altar stone has been inserted into its indent, and it's been draped with the family altar cloth. Lunch has been finished for well over an hour, and all is ready for Mass.

In our line of work, it's good to keep on top of these things. I can't help remembering Thiago's words as we pray. They apply a little less to a farmer than a hunter, but after what happened a few days ago...

Deliver us, O Lord.

JOSHUA

The she-rex enters the hollow a second after Dad flattens himself on the slope and goes motionless.

Uncle Z mutes our throat-mics. "Get the drone back here, Josh. We're going to need more meat."

"We'll lose our eyes—"

He just reaches over and presses the home button, then returns to his watching.

The rocky slope replaces the view of Dad and the nest as the drone zooms back towards us. My heart pounds in my chest as I wonder what's happening up there. Is the rex circling the nest and settling down again, oblivious to Dad's presence? Or is she... I swallow and double-check the drone's speed control, though I know it's on max, then stand up ready to drop down below and fetch more bait.

"Wait!" Uncle Z lunges for the drone controls, sends it shooting up into the air again, his eyes, and his finger, flying to one of the screens. He swears, far worse than normal. As I make out the visual of the heat smudges that have caught his attention, my breath catches in my throat. A pack of Utahraptors are moving our way and not slowly. Have they also caught the scent of that meat—or Dad? Or more likely,

of his ScentBlocker gel, which they still haven't managed to make completely odorless, making it useless against something as smart as a raptor.

"Dad," I murmur, more softly than ever. "Seven Utahraptors approaching from NNW. They'll cut you off from the 'Vi in less than five minutes."

I re-mute the mic and look at Uncle Z. He bites his lip. A cold shiver goes down my spine when he doesn't instantly tell me what to do. But I can make the calculation myself. No way we can re-bait the drone, lure the she-rex away and Dad make it all the way back to the 'Vi before those raptors get here.

From this altitude I'm able to zoom one mobile drone camera back in on Dad. The rex has settled about a third of the way around the nest from him, not too close, but not as far away as she could be. I stare at his motionless figure, wondering what he's thinking. Knowing what he's thinking.

There's no way he can escape a pack of Utahraptors and we can't get the 'Vi any closer to provide cover. Once they cut him off, it's game over. But there's just the tiniest chance that if he makes it over the rim of the hollow immediately the she-rex will stay with her eggs rather than follow and he can make it back to the 'Vi ahead of the raptors.

No chance or a tiny chance. Hunters survive by weighing the odds. 'Cause nothing's a hundred percent safe when you live in a thin metal box surrounded by huge living can-openers. But these odds are…

Dad...

"Josh." Dad's voice is so low I can only just hear him, even with the amplification. "You're the best thing in my entire life...I love you."

My throat's so tight I can barely speak and I'm shaking like a leaf, but somehow I whisper, "Love you, Dad."

Uncle Z stands beside me, absolutely motionless. Doing nothing. Which means there's nothing to be done.

I stare at Dad's huddled form. Is he as scared right now as I am? He just sounds...resolute.

I'm not sure he's really talking to us, but I catch his words. "You're born, you live, you die. Well, Saint Des, here goes nothing..."

He's on his feet and moving, off to a lunging start as he drives his feet into the rocky slope, propelling himself upwards towards the possible safety of that so-close rocky rim.

The she-rex's head swivels at once, her eyes fixing on him as she surges to her feet.

I manipulate the drone control, sending it into a screaming dive. As she takes her first step forward, I batter the drone into the side of her head, frantically trying to distract her.

But a little bird bouncing off her head is of no interest to her when something alive is moving so close to her precious eggs. It's maternal feelings that blaze in her savage eyes, not hunger, as she takes two more strides and...

57

HARRY

Once Mass is over and Father Benedict has been cajoled into renewing the house/vehicle blessing on their HabVi—a renewal he seems to regard as spiritually unnecessary—the hunters go on their way, politely turning down Dad's offer of a night parked within the safety of our twin fence.

"Was that your first Mass?" Father Benedict asks Carol, when he, Darryl, Fred, and I come out after doing the last of the post-Mass tidy-up and find Carol and Sandra relaxing on the patio with a little glass of something. Dad's disappeared into the workshop with Riley to tinker with his latest Sunday project, from the faint clanking sounds. Darryl glances that way then turns back to Carol.

"It was, actually." Carol smiles. "Is that what you're coming to do one week on Saturday?"

"No, that's a marriage blessing. A much simpler ceremony. I hope Mass wasn't too mystifying?"

The marriage blessing was already arranged and people have been invited, so it's going ahead on the planned day, despite the unexpected Sunday Mass.

Carol laughs. "Oh, I can't claim to have understood half of what was going on, but it had a nice vibe to it. You and William will have to explain it to me bit by bit."

"Of course we will. Well, I'll leave you ladies to it."

He turns to my big sis. "Darryl, I've got something for you."

"For *me?*" Darryl's head jerks back slightly in surprise.

"Yes. Come and see."

JOSHUA

I'm at the bottom of the turret ladder, reaching for the door control, my free hand clutching my rifle, when Uncle Z tackles me, slamming me to the floor.

I struggle, fighting him. "Let me go! I've gotta help him! I've got to —"

He pins me down with his greater weight, grabbing my wrists as I try to scratch him. "Josh, calm down! Stop! You can't —" He releases my wrists and grabs my rifle instead, shoving it in my face. "What's this, Josh? Tell me what this is?"

"My rifle! Now let me go!"

He doesn't oblige. "Yeah, a rifle, Josh. A puny little rifle. Not a rex gun. What you gonna do with that, huh?"

I jerk from side-to-side, trying to throw him off. "Fine, let me get the rex gun! Let me get it!"

He rises to his feet this time, but as I dive towards the gun cabinet he grabs me by the collar and shoves my face close to the computer monitor, his free hand swiping quickly at the controls until the drone's view of the nest hollow comes on screen. "Look, Josh! Look! Exactly what do you plan to throw your life away for? Exactly what do you think you can save? His hat? His boot... Argh, no...too late even for..." Uncle Z's voice breaks as we watch the rex...tidying up...after her second, unexpected snack.

I break too. Faced with the absolute proof that it is completely and utterly beyond too late, I crumple to the floor. Uncle Z slumps down with me, holding me tight, and I bury myself in his arms and sob. And sob. And sob.

It feels like the she-rex has just ripped the heart from my chest and the sun from the sky.

Wakefulness comes all at once, in a rush. My heart pounds and cold sweat drenches me. Tension knots all my muscles. Ugh, *outage.* I hate that nightmare worst of all. That true dream. I still miss Dad so much.

But it's just a memory. I let out a long breath, willing my body to relax.

It doesn't. At all.

I come alert, knowing better than to assume I'm just keyed up from the dream. Is there danger?

Carefully, I move my hand to cup the dangling zippers of my sleeping bag, holding them to prevent jingling noises, then I ease up into a sitting position and move to the little screen by the bedroom door. A few taps and I've accessed the main camera network. The living area looks normal and unbreached, the cab and rear pen also. Turret fine. Nothing the north side of the 'Vi—

Everything tilts suddenly, making me drop a hand to the mattress to steady myself. Okay, something large is pushing against us, but is it hostile or just...? I flick through the other exterior cameras until... Hah. No wonder I had that dream.

Mottled grayish-brown rex hide fills the screen as the creature backs into the 'Vi again. More tilting and lurching. But I'm pretty sure it's just using us as a scratching post. Clearly our rear right hand corner is hitting all the itchy spots. No need to make a run for the cab and try to drive off—always dodgy to try and outrun a rex, though occasionally it's necessary. I don't even bother looking at my rifle, there in its night rack on the inside bedroom wall. No use against a rex.

Great. Yawning, I settle down cross-legged in front of the monitor, still very careful not to make any sound. There shouldn't be any interesting smells coming from in here, Dad and Uncle Z were always very strict about odor procedures—and parking precautions—and I don't think I've done anything to disgrace them. So it's just a question of waiting for it to be done and wander off.

A loud roar reverberates through the 'Vi—and from the screen speakers, until I swiftly mute the vehicle's sound system. Huh, a female in season. I guess she's primping ready to impress a potential mate.

She roars again and begins to scratch her breastbone vigorously on the Vi's corner, making us rock some more on our wheels. My amusement at my mental picture of her pre-mating makeover fades as I register how familiar her voice is. Taking in the identifying details as she steps back again, stretching and shaking herself, my humor congeals entirely. Bushy reddish-orange crest feathers. Hide more brown than grey…

You.

My lips form the word as I stare at the she-rex and try not to hate her. Yeah, no wonder I dreamed that dream, with her roaring nearby. Well, I am on the fringe of her territory.

Even after all this time my first instinct is still to slip quietly from the master bedroom, grab the rex gun and have my revenge. If I dug the individually identifiable rex bullet out afterwards, DAPdep would never know who did it. But I made up my mind four years ago not to kill her. Dad wouldn't want me to. He walked right into her nest, after all, it's not like she just ripped our 'Vi open for no reason and ate him.

You're born, you live, you die.

Still, right now suddenly all I can see is her taking those two quick strides, closing her huge jaws around

Dad and biting down, oh, biting down so *hard*, then shaking him viciously and hurling him across the hollow into the sheer side of the cliff.

For the millionth time, I hope that the bite killed him—if not, that hitting the rock at least knocked him out. So he didn't feel what happened next.

My least favorite she-rex reverses up to the 'Vi again and begins rubbing her itchy side. Then her back again. Then her shoulder. Maybe she has parasites.

Eventually, still carefully cupping my dangling zippers, I lie back down, then fold my arms behind my head and resign myself to waiting. Staring at the ceiling in the dim glow of the screen, my thoughts return to Dad. This was always his bedroom—but it was mine, too, until I was old enough to have my rifle beside me at night. Then I moved into the top shelf-bunk in the living area, though for many years Dad still insisted I slept in with him whenever we had a carni'saur or particularly bad tempered herbi'saur in the rear pen—just in case. The master bedroom being much more secure than the cupboard-bunks.

The memories hurt, but that's okay, because it's better I don't drop off again. If I have another nightmare I might start making tasty, unhappy noises in my sleep. I miss Dad—and Uncle Z—but I'm not ready to join them yet. Not if I can help it.

DARRYL

I follow Father Benedict as he heads around the house towards his van, Harry and Fred following close at my heels.

"Why does *Darryl* get something?" complains Fred.

"Avarice is not attractive, young man," returns Father Benedict, deadpan.

Harry snorts in amusement and Fred scowls.

"Really, considering Darryl's never had a proper pet of her own, and I certainly feel like I owe her one after I made such a bad choice with that," Father Benedict shudders, "so-called pussycat, it seems perfectly appropriate she should have something."

"Aw, come on, Father Ben," I say. "You're not still feeling guilty about that, are you? It was a cute-looking little fur ball when you picked it out for me. How were you supposed to know it would grow into...into..."

"The feline equivalent of a psychopath?" Father Benedict grins.

"That about sums it up!" Harry speaks with such fervor, again I hear him shouting at that horrible cat, trying to pretend he didn't have tears on his cheeks as he held up yet another lifeless little—uneaten—body: *if you don't even want to eat it what did you kill it for, you monster!*

Okay, all cats kill things they don't want to eat, but my cat—Dad and Harry never did let me forget it was technically *my* cat—took it to a whole new level. I'd have shot that cat myself, only Dad wouldn't let me, because while it was around we never had a single rat, mouse or rodento'saur on the farm.

"It's not your fault, anyway," I tell Father Benedict. "Dad asked you to bring a kitten for me. He could've chosen it himself. But are you saying you've brought me a pet?"

Oh dear, it's ungrateful of me, but...what if I don't want it? What if it's impractical? Why has he suddenly decided to replace the psycho-kitten, after all these years?

"The cat actually has nothing to do with it," Father Benedict admits. "A brother priest of mine has a little girl in his city parish who's...well, I'm afraid she's sick. Very sick. She's had this little pet of hers for several years that she loves to bits, but no one in her family really wants it. She was fretting so over what would happen to it, Father Pete told her he'd find it a home with another little girl who'd love it as much as she did."

"But...I'm not a little girl, Father Ben!" No, I'm really not. I haven't forgotten the way that young SPARKie private winked at me when we went in-city to get Carol.

65

Father Ben pauses and smiles at me. "Maybe you're not *such* a little girl any more, Darryl, but I know you, and I know you will love this critter and look after it really well, and that's exactly what Father Pete and I promised her."

Worse and worse. Father Ben's promised some poor dying little girl that I will take care of her beloved pet for the rest of its natural life? How long will that be? "But what *is* it, Father Ben?"

Father Benedict smiles. Yep, for all the seriousness, he's enjoying making it a surprise. "I'd really like to take it into the house somewhere quiet and dim before we take the cover off the cage. It's had a stressful week, having to leave its little mistress, being cooped up with just me."

He opens the rear door of his standard diocesan-issue sleeping van—covered in 'I brake for T.rex and archangels' type bumper stickers, with an old two-claw necklace hanging from the rearview mirror—and reaches inside. There's a small, rudimentary living area in the back, nothing like a HabVi and not designed for use unSPARKed, but it gives him a place to stay when parked anywhere that doesn't have a spare room. Country priests like Father Benedict are itinerant, continually on the move from farm-to-farm in order to serve their vast parishes.

The covered cage he lifts out is a good size, far bigger than you'd put a piranha'saur in for travel. A smallish sort of dog would probably fit in it or a monster-cat. It'd better not be another cat. Father Ben likes a joke, but considering how guilty he's always felt about that kitten, it's probably not, thank God. He brushes off our offers to carry it—probably doesn't want us peeking—and bears it quickly inside.

"Uh, bring it up to my room," I say. *Little girl, dying.* I'm stuck with the thing, whatever it is.

Once the cage is on my desk, with the shutters half-lowered to block some of the light, and the boys have been banished to the corner by Father Ben, he starts to ease the cover off the cage. "Okay, Kiko, time to meet Darryl."

I'm dimly aware of Harry and Fred craning their necks behind me, but I'm too focused on the cage interior as it's revealed.

It's a 'saur and it's not nearly as big as the cage suggests. That's my first thought. The critter is barely larger than a piranha'saur; the extra space is for a very long feathery tail. It's some sort of two-legged runner, is my first guess. But as the cover comes off completely and I can see better, I notice the length of the wing-arms—and the extensiveness of the feathers on them. It's a flier. In fact...

Slowly, so as not to alarm the critter, I lean closer to get a better look. Long flight feathers cover the rear legs as well.

"Wow. It's a quadravian, right?" Microraptor, is the scientific name, but nobody uses it because it's too confusing. Even fully carnivorous quadravians are shy and retiring compared to 'normal' raptors AKA killing machines. "A four-winged flier?"

"That's right. It's an omnivore. Tamed from birth, of course, but they're always a bit shy with strangers. Or so Missie informed me. I actually think she was worrying too much—it doesn't seem that frightened to me. But I've followed all her instructions for introducing it to you."

Quadravians were created along with all the other 'saur species during that brief and ill-thought-out explosion of genetic manipulation/restoration back in our grandparents' day—and like most of the other species, enough escaped to form breeding populations. But they've never done well in the wild. The more highly evolved birds out-perform them in practically every way, and they've survived predominantly as pets. They have to be bred instead of simply captured by the crateload like the pesky piranha'saurs and they've gradually been made smarter through that, but...

"You can't give this to me, Father Ben. It's worth a lot of money."

"Missie doesn't care what it's worth. And in the circumstances, nor do her parents. She just needs to know it has a good home."

"Well…it's up to her what she does with it, I guess. Oh, hello? What's your name? Kiko, hmm?" The critter has stopped hiding at the back of the cage and raised its head a little to look at me. Decided I'm not dangerous? "Well, you're extremely pretty, Kiko."

His feathers are glossy and dark, black shot through with iridescent glimmers of green and gold, with a pale grey featherless face and a white crest on top of his head, compact but long feathered, a bit rex-style.

"Omnivore, right? So seeds, fruit, bugs?"

"Frogs and lizards too, in the wild. But any bits of meat are fine. He can have some veggies, as well, but not too much, especially anything high-carb. But Missie prepared a load of care information which I'll give you." Father Benedict gives me a searching look. "Is it okay? Do you like him?"

"He's gorgeous, Father Ben. But…I would've looked after him anyway."

"I know you would, Darryl." He smiles. "That's why I brought him to you. Truth be told…we were running out of time. You know, to track down a little girl who specifically wanted a quadravian. But I really did think you'd love him. Here..." He hands me a small pack of nuts.

I slip one through the bars. "See, we're going to be friends, Kiko."

Kiko shuffles forward and dips his head to grab the nut. Yes, quadravians are very clumsy on the ground, aren't they? Their rear leg feathers get in the way. They don't fly with the up-down wing movement of modern birds, either. Mostly they glide, they're extraordinarily skilled gliders, but when necessary they can achieve brief bursts of self-powered flight, using what I've heard described as a breaststroke motion through the air. Should be interesting to see. But I'd better make sure we're best friends before I take him outside.

I slip a couple more nuts in, and he comes forward to take the last one from me as I poke it through. Yes, he's well-tamed, just a little stressed by all the upheaval in his life, poor thing. "I know how you feel," I can't help muttering.

Father Benedict shoots me a glance, but just says, "I'll be swinging back past here on Tuesday and I'm hoping he'll have taken to you well enough by then that I can get a picture of him with you to send to Missie. So she can see he likes you and that you like him."

"Well, I won't actually try to handle him today," I say. "Better to let him settle in. But I reckon I can get him out tomorrow. Hopefully by Tuesday he'll be pretty comfortable with me."

Kiko suddenly draws back, pulling his wings up around him. Oh, the boys have run out of patience and are creeping forward. Quite frankly, I'm surprised they stayed back this long.

"Wow-ee," says Fred, staring in. "A *quadravian*. I mean, a quadravian! You've got all the luck, Darryl. Wish someone would give *me* a quadravian."

"What, so you can sell it?" quips Harry, though there's a slight note of envy in his voice too.

Fred shrugs and Harry snorts. I roll my eyes.

So does Father Benedict. "And you wonder why I gave it to *Darryl*."

JOSHUA

I'm about to mark the 'Petro's Fabulous Exotics' order complete when I remember how finicky the guy is. Or rather, how tight. He'll take any excuse not to pay the agreed price. I've got plenty of repeat customers who'd cheerfully receive a fresh-caught crateful as seen—as per the contract. But not Petro.

Getting up from the console, I pull on a thick pair of gloves, open the hatch to Small Critter Cage One, reach in and grab a piranha'saur. Shutting the cage securely, I carry my hissing, wriggling handful to the table and examine it carefully under the light as it chomps fiercely on my leather-clad thumb with its needle-like teeth. The piranha-saur, deadly in large numbers, but on its own the ever-popular pet of choice for boys. Go figure.

Okay, so I had one myself, when I was eight. Well-fed and regularly handled, they can actually become quite docile—at least to the one who does the feeding and handling. Many is the city boy who doesn't bother to learn about their pet and—after leaving mom to feed and care for it for weeks—brings a friend home from school and tries to show off the little critter that's tamely following mom around the house and sitting in the washing basket watching her work—or even riding on her shoulder if she's a) tamed it *really* well, b) a natural born optimist or c) rather foolish—only to receive a bleeding finger and red face for their ignorance.

You'd think with them being the ultimate pack hunters they could cope with multiple people feeding them, but they just get confused and don't take to anyone, then. My aptly—if unimaginatively—named 'Snappy' would even bite Dad and Uncle Z if they tried to handle him. But poor Snappy skipped out the open door one day and we had to move on before he got hungry enough to come back. A bad day for both of us. Well, this one's hale and hearty and healthy— though as yet totally untamed. I inject a permanent tag into its shoulder, tap the button to link the tag to the computer entry, then pop '63493' into Cage Two and snag the next one from Cage One. With each one tagged and individually inspected, Petro has a hard time finding anything to complain about. Though he still tries, despite the fact tagging them is supposed to be his job, at his expense.

When all ten of the feisty vermin are checked and tagged—no runts, good—I mark off the order at last and check the remaining contracts. I've already collected a few samples for a Scientific Institute and acquiring a sack of "genuine unSPARKed river pebbles" for a millionaire's garden pond won't take long—I won't bother pointing out that as soon as they go in-city they'll be SPARKed pebbles, the garden designer's choice of word is silly. I need that baby Triceratops for Exception University which, if luck is with me, I should be able to catch by myself, but I also need to cull a pack of carni'saurs causing problems around a small town south of Exception. Allosaurs, big brutes.

Argh, Phil, you useless clunk, why did you have to run out on me right after I took *that* contract? With just me to do the shooting, I'm going to be chasing the critters all over the countryside. I'll focus on that Triceratops calf first, see if I can get one by the time I reach the cull zone, and if I run across another 'Vi in the meantime, well and good, I'll suggest a team-up. I'd rather make no money on the contract than fail to fulfill it. Of course, they'll rib me something merciless for being out here on my own, though they needn't bother. I do know how stupid it is.

An insistent screech issues from Critter Cage Two.

"No, it's not lunchtime yet."

They respond to the sound of my voice with plaintive cries. *Go on, just one finger? Just one? Go on, stick it in.*

Dream on, critters.

DARRYL

"Oh! Oh, darling, it's coming! It's coming right at us!" Carol clutches Dad so tightly I'm surprised he can breathe.

"It's okay, honey. That's one of year-before-last's iggy calves. An iguanodon, y'know? A commonly farmed herbi'saur. They're laid back and easy to care for. Darryl bottle-fed that one. It's weaned, now, but it still likes a little attention from her."

Carol shrinks back into the centre of the feeding trailer, as far from the wide-spaced bars as possible, as the half-grown iggy, with its typical tall, well-built hind quarters and much lower, lighter shoulders and neck, plods towards us on all fours. The highest point of her back already reaches above the top of the trailer's arched grille.

Above us, Kiko's located a good thermal and soars in wide circles, his long, feathered tail rippling in the wind. Quadravians don't like to land on the ground if they can help it, preferring to remain at a sufficient launch height at all times. So with nowhere nearby for him to launch or land other than the tractor and trailer, I've no worries about letting him loose. I'm fairly sure he'd come back now, anyway. We're already pretty attached to each other.

Father Benedict got a great video of him climbing straight out of the cage into my arms when he popped in Tuesday before last. I said a few words to Missie as well, thanks and reassurance to her and praise of Kiko. Hopefully Missie's mind is set at rest.

"This calf's name is Janey," I tell Carol, then glance at Harry, who's up in the tractor cab on lookout. I press the comm button on my ScreamerBand. "All clear, Harry?"

He gives me a double-thumbs up, so I slide out through the bars and get up to the top of the dome before Janey comes alongside. You can't put your hand through solid steel bars to pet something the size of an iggy. They'll crush your hand to pulp without even noticing. But because the grille curves over the trailer in an arch, if you sit on top they can't pin you by accident, except with their head, but you'll only get bruises from that.

"Hello, Janey. Come to say hello?" Her long, flat face looms beside me, and I sense Carol cringing beneath us. I slip my hand round the back of Janey's jaw, into the itchy spot, and scratch hard. She sighs loudly, her beaky mouth parting in enjoyment.

"She's looking to grow into a very fine mare," Dad says. "We'll definitely want to keep her for breeding."

"Hear that, Janey?" I tell my big baby. "You're going to spend your life grazing in well-kept pastures, with your hatchlings at your heels. That's the life for you, isn't it?"

Dad will keep my bottle-fed females if he can, but if one really isn't suitable for breeding it has to go. So Janey's perfect conformation and superb temperament are good news.

"It's so *big*," whispers Carol.

"But harmless," says Dad. "Just don't let them squish you by accident and keep back from their newborns, and you'll find they're one of the gentlest 'saurs around. Look how much she enjoys the attention."

"Janey's not full-grown yet," I can't help saying, still scratching vigorously. "She'll be about half as big again before she's ready to have her first calf. And if she wants to run, she'll go up on her hind legs. Then she's really tall!"

"Wow." Carol speaks weakly, clearly trying to act interested instead of terrified. Though from the crease in her brow, she's picturing Janey, half as big again, up on her hind legs, and her mind is boggling on the image. They are impressive when they decide to run.

Dad suggested Carol come on this little trip around the outer pastures as—though he didn't say it straight-out—a gentle warm-up for this Sunday's trip to the Carrs for a cook-out. We'll be barely twenty minutes driving to their place, but of course we'll be unSPARKed, and we can all tell how nervous she is. After what happened before, it's hard to blame her.

No one goes out-vehicle in the outer pasture without cover from a lookout, because the three wide-spaced strands of our outer fence are there to keep the large herbi'saur stock in rather than keep predators out, T. rex excepted. Of course they *do* keep carni'saurs out, mostly, simply by demarking the human territory, which the smarter carni'saurs learn to avoid. But then there's always the dim and the desperate. As far as they're concerned, my life is in Harry's hands, just as another day his will be in mine.

Dad gives Carol a big tasty branch and coaxes her into holding it up through the bars: "Don't actually put your hand through or she could pin you by accident, just hold it up...that's right..."

Janey begins plucking the leaves from the branch with her beaky mouth. She's so delicate about it Carol actually laughs slightly.

Iguanodons naturally forage among trees and bushes, but they do alright on soft grasses and scrub—at least the ones the modern scientists bred do—which is good since their calm temperament makes them so suitable for farming. Leaves are a treat for them, though.

My ScreamerBand squawks—in one movement, I slip both feet through the bars and drop back into the trailer, whistling to Kiko.

Dad's already pressed his comm button. "What do you see, Harry?"

"Nothing," comes the snarky response, as Kiko dives gracefully through the bars, brakes hard and alights delicately on my shoulder, making Carol jump. "It's time for lunch and I'm hungry."

"*Harry,*" I say reprovingly, rewarding Kiko with some attention for his obedience. "You'll scare Carol."

"I'm okay." Carol speaks bravely, though my sudden return clearly alarmed her.

"Okay, well, Janey's finished her branch," says Dad, though he gives the tractor cab a narrow glare. "It probably is time to head home."

HARRY

"You see, honey," says Dad, as the Carrs' gate swooshes closed behind us. "That's how these little trips usually go."

Darryl nods encouragingly from beside me, and I think Carol musters a smile, but I can't see her face well from the back seat. "Is this...a good fence?"

Dad grins. "Yeah, it's even newer than ours. Maurice owns a rich spread and likes new stuff."

Isn't that the truth! Royce and Bentley and their little sisters get some awesome presents each Christmas. Though...I glance at Darryl...not even they have anything like a quadravian.

"You're not going to drive around it?" Carol's noticed that we're heading straight on down the drive.

"What, the fence? Aw, no, honey. That would be really rude."

"So...we just trust it's okay?"

"That's right, honey. You can't surv…live out here by yourself; you live by trusting each other. Like you trusted the SPARK Brigade when you lived in-city."

"Oh…" Carol's been trusting *someone* as far as fences are concerned her whole life, but clearly didn't realize!

We pull to a halt in the Carrs' perfect white gravel yard and get out, leaving the rifles in the truck, which Dad locks carefully since the youngest little sister is only five. Darryl has Kiko on her shoulder, where he likes to hang out most of the time. The small leash running from his ankle ring to a loop on her jacket is only a precaution, in this unfamiliar place. He already seems to think my big sis is the best thing since electricity—or at least since Missie.

A cat streaks across the yard, making Carol jump. But when Royce's tough old piranha'saur comes tearing after it, Carol screams full out. The piranha'saur stops dead, draws itself up to its full twelve inches—mostly neck and legs—tilts its tiny head back and stares up at her. Its head cocks to one side…

"Don't you even think about it," says Dad. "I will boot you clear over the fence."

The piranha'saur screeches rudely and races off after the cowardly cat. Why couldn't that kitten Father Ben picked for Darryl have grown up into a cat like that? Kiko stares after the tiny carni'saur in an aloof manner, as though knowing he has nothing to fear. Piranha'saurs really are pack hunters and with their itsy-bitsy mouths they can barely kill anything bigger than a mouse by themselves.

"What?" Carol's shaking. "What was it thinking about?"

It was thinking about having a taste. But for once I manage not to blurt that out loud. Kiko, with his beautiful feathers, impeccable manners and tendency to stay wherever Darryl is has caused Carol little stress, but a snappy, featherless piranha'saur fails on all three counts. Hasn't Carol seen one before? I suppose city-folk don't let them outside, and she probably doesn't know many families with young boys. Even in cities kids are more likely to have a dog or something, anyway.

"How did it even get in here?" stammers Carol. "I thought you said the fence—"

"It's just a pet," Darryl says. "It's supposed to be in here."

"They can be a little snappy," Dad warns her. "Like, er, what do you have more commonly in cities? Er, like a Jack Russell. So if it comes near you just push it away with your foot."

"Push it away?"

Dad shoots a doubtful look at her feet. We're all wearing boots, but she's got a pair of little flat shoes on that leave most of the top of her feet bare. Not good.

"William, Darryl, Harry, hello!" Maurice Carr strides out of the house, arms outstretched.

"Yo, Uncle Mau," I greet him, as he and Dad pound each other on the back.

"Hi, Uncle Mau," says Darryl.

He shoots Darryl and me each a big grin, then he steps back. "And this must be the elegant Mrs. Franklyn we've been hearing so much about! But...why, are you alright, Mrs. Franklyn?"

"She just met, what's the beast called, Harry?"

"Reagan," I supply.

"Yeah, I don't think she was expecting a carni'saur to be loose. I should've warned you, honey. Sorry."

"It's a *carni'saur*?"

I choke slightly and turn away to hide my expression. Now *Dad's* gone and put his foot in it for once!

"Oh, it's no different than a dog, honey. A very *small* dog. You need about fifty of them before they're really *dangerous*." Dad sounds a bit desperate. "And no one *ever* keeps more than one."

Yeah, soon as you have two of the things together they won't bond with you for love or money and those nasty pack hunting instincts start to kick in. And whatever Dad says about fifty—I wouldn't want to fend off *twenty* myself—you'd know about it if even two of the things started biting, biting, biting on your hand in a feeding frenzy.

"Yes, not to worry, Mrs. Franklyn," says Uncle Mau. "Reagan belongs to my son Royce. Just leave him to his own devices and he won't bother you."

Unless you smell so deliciously frightened. Reagan will definitely bite Carol, if he gets a chance. Darryl gives me a meaningful look. I roll my eyes and nod. I'll ask Royce to lock Reagan up, soon as I see him. Carol's just calming down a little bit about the 'saurs. I mean, she even fed Janey the other day. Guess we don't want her getting nipped by that cranky old critter.

"But *Darryl*, I say..." Uncle Mau has been eyeing Kiko and now bends for a better look. "What in the world do you have there? Is it actually... yes, a quadravian. Well, that's *fancy*! That your reward for shooting so straight a couple of weeks back, is it? I didn't even know you hankered for one."

Dad goes slightly red—embarrassed at the implication he might have splurged so lavishly?

Darryl just shakes her head. "No, nothing to do with that. It's very sad, actually—a little girl called Missie owned him, but she's...very, very sick...so Father Benedict brought him to me so she wouldn't worry about his future."

83

Uncle Mau whistles. "Well, I guess just occasionally all that praying brings you some return."

Darryl rolls her eyes at that while Dad punches Uncle Mau in the shoulder. "Pagan!"

Carol's eyes widen in alarm, making Uncle Mau roar with laughter and whack Dad on the back. "Relax, Mrs. Franklyn. Your husband and I have grown up our whole lives on these two farms side-by-side. Take more than that to offend *me*. I *am* an awful pagan, and I don't much care who knows it."

"One day, Mau," says Dad. "God'll get you in the end."

"Dead or alive, eh?"

"Well, I hope it'll be while you're still alive or you'll be in for it."

Uncle Mau just laughs, shepherding us around the back of the house to where his expensive retro grill sits on his extravagantly large area of decking.

JOSHUA

Right, time to get those stupid "unSPARKed" pebbles. I've not caught my Triceratops calf yet, but this stream is perfect. I've parked as close to the edge as I can safely get. If I had an assistant this would be easy money. As it is, it's the most risky contract of them all.

84

Two sacks and a shovel wait down by the side door. I'll fill the sacks quick as I can, then clean and sort the pebbles back inside the 'Vi until I've got one sack of good ones. I inspect the surrounding landscape one more time with my binoculars and re-check each screen. The heat sensors are all set. Anything larger than a very small velociraptor will trip the alarm. I've been monitoring the area for an hour, and I've seen no hint of carni'saurs. Hopefully I can fill the sacks in only five minutes, but if I can't, I'll work on a standard 2:1 ratio, ten minutes up in the turret, watching, for every five minutes outdoor work. Slow, but the only way to cut the risk of solo outdoor work to something halfway acceptable.

Right. If I wait any longer I'm just stalling.

I slide down the ladder from the turret and go to the side door. A quick check of the screen, and I let the door slide open. Usually I like a bit of outdoor work, but *usually* I've got cover. Make that, *always* got cover.

Grabbing the sacks and shovel, I drop lightly to the ground. I don't have my rifle and that's deliberate. It will simply get in the way and slow my work, and if something dangerous does come along my best chance is to get back inside the 'Vi, not get tempted into making some suicidal stand.

I slither down to the water's edge, my boots splashing into the stream. Grabbing a pebble from the streambed, I take a quick look, just to check. Yep, round, smooth, exactly what they want.

The first few shovelfuls are awkward to get in, until the sack is full enough to stay open by itself, then things speed up. Still, my five minute alarm bleeps just as I'm putting the first shovelful into the second sack. Sighing, I heave the full sack onto my back and stagger up the slope to the 'Vi, sling it in and climb in after.

Up to the turret, where I give the landscape a thorough going over for ten minutes, sending my drone further out to re-check for more distant heat signatures. I locate many large grazers, but no carni'saurs.

The ten minute bleep.

Out I go again. Feet in the cold stream, I pick up the shovel and finish filling the second sack. It doesn't take long and my five minute bleep hasn't yet sounded as I heave it up the slope and deposit it in the 'Vi.

Now I just need my shovel.

I've almost got to the stream when the heat sensor's *dong* issues from my ScreamerBand. It's probably just one of those grazers wandering closer—but I turn and jog straight back up the bank, reaching the 'Vi in moments. I'll make *sure* of that and *then* I'll get the—

I catch movement from the corner of my eye, something *fast*. If it's a raptor, they can jump twenty feet and it's already in range.

I bend my own legs and make a massive upward leap for the doorway—my feet just come down in the 'Vi...I can feel that *fastness* shooting up behind me as I hit the close pad and throw myself further inside.

Only to pitch forward on my face as something grabs my foot and yanks me backwards.

DARRYL

"He won't come!" ten-year-old Royce mutters to Harry. "He knows I'm going to put him in his cage."

"Well, for Pete's sake don't let him get near my step-mom, okay?"

"I'll try, but you know how fast he can move!"

"Seriously, Dad will probably *stomp* on him!"

"Well, that would make Porscha happy."

I can't help smiling at that resigned mutter. Royce's tom-boy sister Porscha, eight-years-old, has wanted a piranha'saur for about three years. But Reagan was here first, so she won't get one until he drops dead—or bites the wrong person. If he goes for Carol, this really could be Porscha's lucky day.

I've never been that crazy about the snappy beasts myself. Though Dad says they make good children's pets precisely because you get back what you put in. You want a calm, tame, loyal one, you've got to give it your time and attention. Teaches a young kid more than a dog, which will remain slavishly devoted to you however poorly you train it, that's what Dad says.

But it's hard to believe they ever really *love* you. I stroke Kiko's neck as his head turns this way and that, watching everything in these new surroundings closely. He's wrapped his long tail around my neck for reassurance, like a soft, feathery scarf, but he's bonded tightly enough with me that he's happy enough.

Let's face it, Kiko's affection probably stems mostly from his stomach as well, but he's still much nicer to have around, in my opinion. It's clear he's been a treasured pet. He's extremely calm and exceptionally responsive. Someone's trained him really well and I guess I know who. I offer up another prayer for Missie and her family, as I've been trying to do whenever I think about her.

Maurice goes to reclaim his spatula from Riley, who's been minding that blazing state-of-the-art grill. Riley yields it with a trace of reluctance, but he also grew up right here with Dad and Maurice, and knows not to come between the loud, stocky man and his latest toy. Carol has already gravitated to Sandra. From the fact Dad's sticking by her side instead of joining the steak flipping/grill admiration party, he knows Reagan is still at large. If only she wasn't so nervous. Though that little critter has a nasty sense of humor at the best of times, if one can call it that, and always makes a beeline for strangers. More fun than chasing the cat for the millionth time, I suppose.

I have a sudden image of Carol perched elegantly on a tree branch, staring down at Reagan leaping and hissing around the trunk, and barely manage not to snort with laughter. Of course, piranha'saurs are good climbers, so it wouldn't help, even if she managed to get up there without messing up her hair, bless her!

"Hey, what's the joke?" asks Harry, abandoning his whispered conference with Royce.

"Uh, nothing. Where's Fred?"

"With Bentley, I guess. I haven't seen either of them yet. They'll be here fast enough when they hear about Kiko."

The Carrs' oldest child, Bentley, fifteen, is pretty thick with fourteen-year-old Fred, though they tend to let thirteen-year-old Harry tag along with them. Bentley, Royce, Porscha, and little Lotus, those are the Carr children—yeah, Maurice has a terrible sense of humor when it comes to names, which their mom shared. She died two years ago, poor kids. They're looked after by a succession of expensive nannies from the city. They've yet to get one to stay long-term. I think it's mainly the whole out-city life thing, though

Maurice does have a reputation for being a demanding employer. He's a pretty strict dad, too, but there's no doubt he loves all four of them, and they adore him.

"Why don't we find them and form a hunting party?"

"Heh? Oh, *Reagan*. Come on, we don't need to go looking. We've got the bait right here." He nods at Carol, now chatting happily to both Sandra and the latest nanny.

"Yes," I tell Harry, my tone getting a little too patient, "but by the time he gets here it will probably be too late!" I just manage not to add 'clunk-head'.

Harry makes a face. "Yeeeee-as. That's true. Okay, let's go."

JOSHUA

I grab the edge of a unit as I fly past it. My arms get a terrible jolt but I hang on tight, looking back.

A Dakotaraptor's got my foot. The door has closed on its neck, mercifully stopping it getting its body through or my belly would be slit open already. But it's got my foot in its mouth. The steel toe cap in my boot is protecting me, but I'm not sure it'll hold if it really bites down.

It yanks again, shaking me, trying to drag me closer so it can transfer its grip higher. I cling on for my dear life, drawing my free foot back and kicking its nose as hard as I can. The eye would be more delicate, but I'd have to put my leg within range of its teeth, doing its work for it.

Jerking back slightly, it shakes its head, not liking the blows, then throws its head to the side, pulling so hard it almost gets me loose. I manage to slip one arm right inside the cupboard, anchoring myself more securely, and look for a weapon.

There! The spade I rejected in favor of the scoopier shovel still leans against the cupboard side, only feet away. I stretch desperately but I can't reach it.

The raptor starts pulling hard again and for a moment I concentrate on hanging on and raining kicks on its nose. It's snarling, its eyes spearing me with loathing.

The loathing's mutual.

It eases up after a particularly good kick, so I quickly free one arm again and punch the side of the cupboard as hard as I can.

The spade rocks.

I punch again.

It topples, falling...yes! It lands closer to me. I stretch...raptor yanks...but my fingertips are on the blade; I manage to grip it...draw it closer...get my hand around the handle, *yes!*

Wielding it one-handed, I swing it as hard as I can, aiming for the raptor's eye. It jerks its head to the side, managing to avoid the blow striking home, but the edge of the spade still smacks into its cheek with a resounding thud. It yanks at me again, shaking me, spoiling my aim, but I swing the spade again, *hard*, and again, *hard*...

I still don't connect with the eye, but it's only a matter of time, and the screeching raptor's bright enough to realize that trapped as it is, it doesn't entirely have the upper claw.

Swing, thud, screech!

Swing, thud, screech!

The raptor's struggling, now, struggling to escape. My arm aches from wielding the heavy spade at such an angle, but I mustn't show the tiniest sign of weakness.

Swing, thud, screech!

Swing—

The blow smacks into the door as it slides closed. The raptor's finally managed to pull its head back outside. I lunge forward, swinging the spade—much more gently—to connect with the lock button. Just in case.

Then I drop the spade and lie there on the floor, panting and shaking.

A blasted garden pond.

I almost died for someone's blasted garden pond. Unbelievable.

But after I've lain there shaking for a while more, I can't deny the truth. I almost died because I was too impatient to wait until I'd replaced Phil. That's the truth. Was avoiding two more days in-city really worth my life?

"Oh, Joshua," I prophesy to the ceiling above me. "Your city-phobia will be the death of you."

HARRY

Groaning and rolling their eyes, Fred and Bentley agree to help us, probably because Darryl announces that no one is getting to do anything with Kiko until Reagan's locked away and they're dead keen to see her new pet fly. "Like nature's very own drone," as Bentley puts it. Porscha and Lotus come along as well, though they're so busy gazing up at the glossy quadravian I doubt they're going to be much help.

"Why'd you even have to let him out today?" grumbles Fred, as he, Darryl, Royce, and I poke our way through a dung heap, while Bentley searches the gap between two barns with the two younger girls.

"Why shouldn't I have let him out?" retorts Royce. "He's only a piranha'saur, for crying out loud! Anyone would think we had a velociraptor on the loose."

93

"*No one* keeps a pet velociraptor," says Fred, quite unnecessarily.

The dog-sized velociraptor is every bit as vicious as its larger cousins, and though all raptors are somewhat trainable—by one person—if raised from hatching, only the military are allowed to use them as guard animals. And even they stick to the smaller velociraptors. Easier to put down if the person they're imprinted on is so inconsiderate as to drop dead.

"This is a total waste of time," says Fred. "I bet the little vermin is already—"

Kiko cocks his head suddenly—an instant later a shriek echoes from the decking behind the farmhouse. Royce sprints in that direction, clearly eager to save his pet if he can.

Darryl sighs. "Well, we did our best." She gives Kiko a quick scratch, as though rewarding his alertness, little as it helped, and jogs after Royce.

When we come panting up to the decking Carol stands on a garden bench, shaking, while angry noises come from beneath the big domed grill lid Dad holds clamped down on the wooden boards.

"Royce, lock that beast up," orders Uncle Mau. "It just tried to take a chunk out of Mrs. Franklyn, here."

"Sorry, Dad," mutters Royce. He shrugs off his jacket, holds it at the ready, and nods to Dad, who lifts the domed lid. Royce manages to chuck the jacket over Reagan and bundle him up.

"You really need that jacket?" Dad's frown is disapproving—he clearly thinks Royce hasn't been looking after Reagan enough.

Royce looks offended. "Only to get him out! If I stick my hand under there he won't check whose it is before he sinks his teeth in!" He speaks soothingly to his wriggling handful, then untangles the jacket from over the little 'saur's head. Reagan lets out his equivalent of a stream of swearwords, but makes no attempt to bite as Royce carries him away.

"Where did you all go?" asks Dad. "Food looks about done."

Darryl shrugs, making Kiko hook a wing claw in her hair for balance. "Looking for Reagan. I'm glad he didn't actually bite Carol."

"Yeah, well, let's just say I was expecting him." Dad helps Carol down from the bench—she glows adoringly at him. She doesn't actually gasp, 'my hero', but I have to look away as she glues her lips to his. Yuk!

"Mrs. Franklyn, allow me to give you my personal assurance that whenever you visit in future, that nasty beast will be locked in its cage." Uncle Mau is working damage control already. "Now, allow me to help you to the first burger."

Carol gets fussed over, which she seems to enjoy, but soon we're all digging in.

"So what do you think of William's iggys, then, Mrs. Franklyn?" says Uncle Mau. "I hear you went out to see them."

"Do call me Carol..."

"Carol. Nice name, Carol. All those positive associations of Christmas, without being so gauche as the name 'Christmas', eh?"

What does 'goosh' mean? Well, I don't want to say anything in front of Bentley and Fred; I can ask Darryl later.

"Flirting with William's new wife while he's holding one of these stupidly over-sized steak forks of yours, Mau?" sniggers Riley.

Uncle Mau just chuckles, while Carol tries to answer the original question politely. "I, uh, did feed one. They've very...very...uh...*large.*"

"Iggys, large?" Uncle Mau laughs outright. "Phewee, Carol, iggys are one of the smallest of William's 'saur-stock. I've got nothing smaller. Do you know how big a full-grown edmontosaur is, for example? Let alone a—"

"Come on, Mau, all in good time," interrupts Dad.

Carol's eyes are wide.

"Well, *this* is certainly a very fine beast." Obligingly changing the subject, Uncle Mau looks Kiko over again. "But perhaps not to your step-mom's taste, eh, Darryl?"

Darryl smiles. "Oh, even—" She breaks off as though swallowing her tongue and two spots of red appear on her cheeks.

But Carol just smiles at her. "*Even Carol likes Kiko?*" Darryl goes brick red. "It's okay, sweetie. I'm downright petrified of 'saurs and there's no point pretending otherwise. But I never feel like little Kiko wants to eat me, so I don't mind him. I mean, I wouldn't want him *on* me."

"Can I hold him now, Darryl?" begs Porscha.

"Let's finish eating first." Darryl clearly wants all her attention free in case she has to break up a tug-of-war over her exotic four-winged pet.

"Now, Mrs. Franklyn... Sorry, *Carol*," Uncle Mau is still being very polite to her. "How about you talk your husband into selling me his little field, eh?"

Carol glances from person-to-person. She can tell from the smiles and chuckles that it's a joke, but of course she doesn't get it. "You want to buy it?"

"Does he!" laughs Dad. "Yes, he wants to buy it. That field would link together the two parts of his holding."

Carol frowns, "Then if it's such a little field, why not let him?"

Everyone roars with laughter.

97

"Because it's not a *little* field at all," says Darryl. "It's a massive pasture, and it's the best pasture on our farm. What's more, it's the best pasture anywhere in about a thousand mile radius. He knows he's not getting it, it's just a running joke."

Carol looks at Uncle Mau again, who's grinning hugely. "Oh, I see. Yes, of course you wouldn't want to sell something like *that*. I don't know a lot about real estate, myself. My brother does, it's his trade."

"He an estate agent?" asks Sandra.

"Land auctioneer, actually. He does a lot of valuation work, some selling."

"You can ask William to sell me that nice acreage on my side of the farm, while you're at it, then," puts in Riley, "and your brother can handle the sale, eh?" He winks at Dad, who grins.

"I'm not selling either and you both know it."

Riley sighs. "Yeah, don't I. Of course, the problem nowadays when entire family farms go under the hammer is that those rich carni'saurs from the city buy them up, but they don't want to farm them themselves. They just put tenants in to farm them for them. Ends up with farm folk who want to buy their own farm unable to afford one and stuck as tenants."

"That's not new, Riley," says Dad. "Been going on since year one."

"There has been a surge of interest in land ownership in the last decade, though," says Uncle Mau. "I've had approaches from city investors. That's how they view it, an investment."

"I think for a long time they didn't want to think about 'out here' at all," says Sandra. "But the more of them get wise to the fact that the land is still worth money and that they don't have to farm it themselves, the more its value rises."

I turn my attention to my burger as the boring and familiar arguments go around. Soon Darryl's finished eating and Kiko is being given ample opportunity to show how polite and well-socialized he is.

He doesn't let Darryl—or himself—down. More than ever I can't help wishing Father Benedict had given him to *me*—but I'm still glad to have him in the family, period.

JOSHUA

Eventually, I ease stiffly up into a sitting position. My left leg aches fiercely, all the muscles yanked and strained, and my shoulders and arms only feel marginally better. My back muscles haven't enjoyed being in the middle of that little tug o' war, either. My hands are sore too...when I look at them, I find that my knuckles and the heels of my hands are scraped and bleeding from scrabbling at metal.

My precious left foot is still attached, so I can't complain. But when I bend my knee and draw the foot closer to examine it, a much sharper pain stabs through it. Is it broken? Crushed? Or...

Oh. Impaled? A nasty great raptor fang sticks from my boot leather, just about where the steel toecap would run out. I resist the temptation to grab it and pull it straight out and maneuver to my feet instead. Hopping to the first aid cabinet to avoid putting weight on the foot—which may be broken, crushed *and* impaled, for all I know—I remove anything I might need, then lower myself back down onto the floor, where I'll be able to reach my foot more easily. After putting everything handy, I finally take hold of the tooth and draw it...ooooooouch...out.

Putting it aside, I quickly ease the boot off—ouch— peel my bloody sock off and take a look. Yeah, the fang got me good. I never even felt it during that life-and-death struggle, not that worrying about it then would have helped.

I staunch the bleeding with sterile wadding, inject a shot of antisepsis serum directly into the nearby flesh, and spray it thoroughly with anti-septic before finally sprinkling it with clotting agent. That stops the bleeding fast enough. Once I've cleaned my foot with sterile odor wipes, I apply a hunk of artificial skin over the wound to hold it all closed, keep it clean and seal in blood smell. So that's that.

Time to find out what else is wrong. Gingerly, I flex the foot. Ooh. Doesn't feel good, but...probably not actually broken. Severely wrenched around. Stressed joints and sprained muscles. But no smashed bones? No. It moves too well.

That's a relief. I'd better find my spare boots.

First, I pick up the bloody tooth and examine it. Old and rotten. Yep, it fits with the impression I got from what I saw of the critter. An old male. Probably a matriarch's mate who left the pack with her when she lost her position. Quite likely she's now dead and he's completely alone, and when pack hunters end up alone they grow desperate pretty quickly. Is he still lurking out there? I need to retrieve my shovel; maybe I could dispatch him at the same time. I won't even need to fill in a cull report—I can just show them my boot!

Boots. Yeah, boots first. I get to my good foot again and put the first aid stuff away—bloody wipes straight into the incinerator—then hop to my bedroom and haul myself up using mostly my arms—owwww— until I can get in and retrieve socks and spare boots from the interior cupboards. Getting down and putting them on isn't very pleasant either.

Why don't you remember how unpleasant the next time you're tempted to act like a complete clunk-headed idiot, huh?

Transferring a piranha'saur to a small shoulder cage, I sling my rifle over my other aching shoulder and haul-hop my way painstakingly up the ladder to the turret. The cage shoved out of the way under the console, I check the surrounding landscape carefully for threats. The large herbi'saurs still graze quietly, unconcerned by the single raptor lurking nearby. Yeah, he's still out there. There's the heat smudge on the display. Probably still hoping to have me for dinner.

Where was he earlier? In a cave, maybe, or behind a large rock at an angle the drone's heat sensor couldn't catch. Or maybe quite a lot further away and he caught my scent and came running full-tilt. No amount of checking beforehand is foolproof, that's why you always have cover when you go outside. *Hear that, Joshua? You should have cover.*

Okay, okay, I learned my lesson. Now, let's get my shovel back.

I bring the drone in, then re-deploy it, now carrying a spiderline, which I manage to hook over the handle of my shovel easily enough. The winch hauls the tool into the open rear pen and I seal the door. One shovel acquired.

Now for one starving raptor.

I glove up and take out the piranha'saur, crimping a leg ring onto its ankle and attaching a secure line. Then I raise one narrow window and let the critter slip through the bars and sit out there on the roof, biting furiously at its restraints. The other windows I leave down, since the tinted surface will hide me from view. After getting rid of the gloves and checking my rifle is ready, I slip off the safety catch.

It's not a long wait. Barely minutes pass before that raptor-shaped smudge starts moving. It's going so fast when it arrives I don't get a shot until it leaps up onto the roof and bears down on the oblivious piranha'saur. As I take the necessary moment to make sure the muzzle is between the bars it sees me through the open window—yeah, it's old and rail thin and it certainly recognizes a gun, because it leaps sideways so fast my shot only grazes it.

Moving swiftly but calmly, I raise more windows, then bring the rifle up—through bars, check—and settle the crosshairs on that rapidly retreating figure. Steady, steady...squeeze.

The rifle cracks; the raptor barks, stumbles and topples. I'm pretty sure it's a clean kill, but I put another bullet into the now stationary target that's its head, to be sure. For its sake—and for mine.

Hauling the recalcitrant piranha'saur in, I return it to its carry-cage, then hop painfully back down the ladder. Piranha'saur—back into the pen with the others. HabVi—moved a hundred yards north and reversed up to the dead raptor. And then back to the turret, though I'm gasping with pain by the time I get up there. My hands shake with exhaustion as I put a second bullet in the critter's head from this absolutely certain range, then deploy the drone and the spiderline again. Around the raptor's ankle. Operate the winch. Seal the doors.

Now I've just gotta skin it, butcher its meat for the piranha'saurs, freeze or seal up what I want, dump what I don't, wash out the pen, take a shower and drive at least a short distance away. Then, free of the scent of blood and unlikely to attract something the size of a T. rex or spinosaur that could actually seriously endanger the 'Vi, I can collapse and get some rest.

Come to think, isn't there some religious thing about not working on Sunday? Maybe I made St. Des mad by shoveling those pebbles.

Well, too late now. I've got a carcass to deal with.

DARRYL

"Today's the day, Kiko," I tell my feathered friend as I head out into the yard.

Kiko gives an inquiring screech.

"The marriage blessing. This afternoon." There's something very final about it, somehow, not that Dad and Carol aren't already properly married in the eyes of the Church.

"Darryl?" Carol leans out of the door. "Don't you need a coat on? It's so early, still."

A trace of irritation stirs at this intervention, but an odd warmth in my chest too. "Uh, I'm off to walk the mammal-stock pastures, Carol. I'll get warm really fast."

"Oh. Right." She smiles, I smile back, and she disappears back inside.

I like Carol. My nerves about today aren't because I don't like her. Dad's right, she's a very nice person, though hopeless with 'saurs. And she and Dad are head over heels for each other. Kind of sweet and nauseating, all at once.

But it still feels like the blessing this afternoon, in an illogical sort of way, will make these changes in my life permanent. And that's scary.

Why should it be, Darryl, if it's a good change?

I head towards the pastures as fast as I can, partly because it's cold and partly because Harry's taken on all the standard pre-breakfast chores so I can inspect the pastures now and we can all have more time to get ready for the big event. The Wahlburgs, Carrs, and Swayles are all coming, along with several other local families.

Carol got the designs for her two capes done the previous week—I'm more and more impressed by her efficiency—and sent the stuff off to the tailors. She hasn't designed the rest of the collection yet, since she spent most of this week cooking for today. Dad assured her no one would expect anything very fancy, but didn't try too hard to discourage her. She was having far too much fun.

Kiko climbs up onto my head, front wings spreading as he tests the breeze.

"Want a lift?" I hold out my hands. He scrambles straight into them and I toss him up into the air as high as I can. He soars overhead, lands high on a barn, jumps and glides again—lands on the next barn. Thermals aren't great today, clearly.

That's proved when he returns to my shoulder once I'm out in the pasture, instead of staying aloft. I work quickly, checking fences, troughs, and feeders, and looking over each bunch of cows as Harry turns them out. They're all moving well, except one we already know is lame.

When I get to the far side of the farm, Dad's truck is still parked out near the fence. Hasn't he moved on to other things by now? He went out much earlier than normal to check the fence this morning. He must be replacing something. I'll head over there and join him. Maybe I can fetch something for him and speed the repair up, otherwise he can give me a lift back for breakfast and that'll save a few more minutes.

There's no sign of Dad as I approach the farm truck, though. Maybe the fence is fine and it's the truck that's broken down, and he's walked back to get something.

"Dad?" He might just be crouched down behind it. Probably is, actually, since the driver's door is open.

"Dad?"

I walk around the hood and my throat constricts, my heart hammering in my chest.

Deep claw marks score the side of the vehicle, the door, the roof...

A puddle of some dark liquid pools on the grass...

I dash forward and look inside.

More blood splashed across the seats. Rips in the upholstery.

But no Dad.

I spin around, my eyes searching. Dad?

Nothing.

Lifelong training finally catching up with the shock, I press the breach button on my ScreamerBand and leap over the bloodied driver's seat into the passenger side, pulling the door shut behind me, Kiko's screech of alarm barely audible over the breach alarm from my wrist. I mute it quickly, move Kiko to the dashboard—"Stay, Kiko!"—and start climbing around the truck, peering out of the windows. *Dad, where are you?*

"*Dad? Darryl?*" It's Harry.

"Harry, where are you?"

"I'm in Barn B. I locked it down, I'm safe."

"Do you know if Carol is in the house?"

"As far as I know, but I don't *know*. Dad, what's going on?"

Silence. No reply from Dad. I'm gasping for breath, my hands shaking. Why doesn't he answer?

"Darryl?" Harry's voice goes high and nervous. "Darryl, where's Dad? Where are *you*?"

"I..." My voice shakes. "I..." I can't get the words out.

"Ryl? Ryl, calm down. Calm down and talk to me. Please?" Harry's voice trembles.

"I-I'm at Dad's truck, Harry." My voice comes out all strangled. "But he's not here. There's...there's blood and claw marks, Harry."

"Outage." Harry breathes it so softly I barely hear.

108

I struggle to think. I'm the one with a vehicle; I've got to search for Dad. But first...

Everyone accounted for.

I press my comm button again. "Carol? Carol, where are you? Carol, please push the green button on your wristband and talk to me. I need to know where you are."

Silence. Blast. Has she completely frozen up? "D-D-Darryl?"

Is she hyperventilating? Oh no, she must've heard what I told Harry. Somehow I manage to speak very slowly and firmly. "Carol, are you in the house?"

"Yes..."

"Okay, Carol, I need you to walk to the House Control and lower the shutters. You remember Da...you remember we showed you how to do that, right?"

"Is...is...there...s-s-s-something...in...h-h-here?"

"Carol, listen to me. There is *nothing* in the house, okay?" Lord, let that be true! "But I need you to walk to House Control and lower the shutters. Then I can go and help Dad deal with this, okay?

"Where's...where's William?"

"Carol, the best way you can help him is by *lowering the shutters*, okay?" *Please, God, let her just...*

Harry chips in again. "Shall I—"

"No!" I don't even let him finish. "Follow the rules, Harry!" No way am I letting him sprint across that yard to the house just because Carol's too scared to walk down the hall. Those marks in the truck door weren't made by anything as large as an allosaur and the house windows are supposed to be raptor-proof, so Carol's probably safe anyway.

"I-I'm...walking...down the...hall..." Carol's whisper comes from my wrist.

"That's great, Carol. That's great. Just head right on to the House Control. Are you there?"

"I-I can't remember which—"

"The red button with the square shapes on it. Just push that once."

"Oh! They closed!"

"Good. Right, you're fine, Carol. Just sit tight and...and try to relax."

Stupid words. How can she relax after what she just heard me say? But what else can I tell her?

"Darryl, please go and find Dad." Harry's voice squeaks.

"I'll find him! You just stay put." I look around the truck. I'll have to sit in the driver's seat, blood or no blood, but is...yes! Dad's rifle is there by the handbrake. He always takes it when checking the fence, in case he has to go between-fence or switch an outer section off for repair.

But if it's here, he hasn't got it with *him*.

I try not to think about that big pool of blood under the door. A little blood goes a long way. If he's only lost what's splashed around here, that won't have killed him. A little voice says, *not on its own*, but I ignore it.

But where *is* he? Where could he have hidden, out here? *Or been dragged?* No, I'm not thinking that. I check the back, then after a careful look around outside, I open the door and stick my head beneath the truck, but he's not under there either. Door securely closed again, I quarter the surrounding area slowly and carefully with my eyes, searching for any clue about where to look first.

"Kiko, shsss. Just sit."

Finally, my eyes fix on the closest bit of fence. Is that...?

I start the truck, put it in gear and move it right alongside the fence and look more closely.

There's a hole. A very small one. A patch of disturbed and pushed aside wires. Two snapped. All smeared with blood.

A similar hole in the outer fence.

But... Something large enough to make those claw marks simply could not have got through a hole that size, right? Even leaving aside the electricity. Let alone dragged Dad back through after it. Right? This doesn't make sense.

Never mind for now how it got in. Find Dad!

I put the truck in gear again and drive around the farm, between every barn, circling every trough, every tank, every place Dad could have tried to take shelter from a smallish Dakotaraptor—I'm sure that's what made the claw marks.

Nothing.

Finally I drive the fence, looking for another entry point.

Nothing.

I end up back in front of that tiny, bloody hole.

Maurice's truck pulls up behind me only minutes later. The Wahlburgs and Swayles arrive soon afterwards, all responding to our breach alarm.

We drive the farm again, all four vehicles, but find no sign of Dad—or of danger. So we get out, take our guns and walk it on foot, all of us, Maurice and Bentley and Royce, Riley and Sandra and Fred, all the Swayle girls who're old enough to be out with a rifle, plus Harry and I.

We search every last corner of the farm.

And we end up right back at that fence.

Staring at that tiny, blood-stained hole.

Having found *nothing*.

===+===

Look out for unSPARKed 3
PANIC!
Out Now!

If you have enjoyed this unSPARKed story, would you consider leaving a review at your favorite retailer?
Thank you!

unSP🔥RKED

Prequels

BREACH!

CORINNA TURNER

CARNEGIE MEDAL NOMINEE

DON'T MISS

BREACH!

An unSPARKed Prequel

Set 19 years before A TRULY RAPTOR-OUS WELCOME.

HE PROTECTS PEOPLE FOR A LIVING. BUT WILL A MISTAKE COST HIM HIS CHILD'S LIFE?

Eighteen-year-old Isaiah and his older brother Zechariah are professional hunters, earning their living culling and capturing some of the most dangerous predators ever to walk the planet.

When an out-of-control T. rex breaches a tourist resort Isaiah and Zech must act fast to save lives.

Little does Isaiah know that a testy T. rex and three packs of hungry raptors will soon be the least of his problems. A much-regretted New Year's Eve misadventure is about to cause a very different kind of breech—and change both their lives for good.

OUT NOW!

Read a SNEEK PEEK!

unSeen

Find out more at: www.UnSeenBooks.com

BREACH!

Beep.

Beep.

Beep.

The persistent noise draws me sluggishly from sleep, dumping me not into full wakefulness but into a stomach-clenching memory of that morning—an alarm clock waking me, my head thumping, no idea where I was, panic quickly giving way to a bone-deep regret and a shame that still clings to me like dirt...

Argh, that was over two months ago, just after my eighteenth birthday. Late February now and I've put it behind me. Lesson learned and all that. Yeah, I'm good at learning from my mistakes. If I wasn't, I'd have been eaten by now.

And that beep isn't some city dweller's alarm clock; it's the HabVi's console. In fact, it's—

I sit up so fast I bang my head on the roof of my little overCab bedroom—this is the spacious "Master" bedroom in newer Habitation Vehicles, but in our old banger it's almost as pokey as the shelf bunk in the living area, where I slept for five years.

Breach alarm. But not *our* breach alarm. Grabbing my rifle from alongside my sleeping bag, I still check the dim screen beside the bunk door, but the living area looks normal. Jumping out without even glancing at the footholds, I land easily on the metal floor and dart to the console, pulling a sweater on.

Yes, a nearby farm has a breach. In fact—*Oh no!*

I slap my hand on the "open" button of the cab bedroom without knocking. "Zech!" The door slides open and I dive into the driver's seat, dumping my rifle beside me and whacking the sleeping bag swaddled feet on the seat-bed. "Zech, can't you hear the alarm? Get up!" I open the cab's solid metal shutters, raise the stabilizers, and deploy the mirrors with three quick button flicks, then turn the ignition key. "There's a breach nearby!"

"All right, all right, Isaiah." A huge yawn, and my older brother's tousled black hair appears at the top of his sleeping bag, along with a glimpse of brown skin and sleepy brown eyes very like my own.

"It's that *tourist resort*, Zech!"

"Argh, *outage!*" Zech jack-knifes into a sitting position, still swearing. Really swearing. I know how he feels, but...

"Zech!" I glance meaningfully at our little statue of Saint Desmond on the dashboard. "Now, seriously?" He'll really cheese Saint Des off just when we're heading into a breach situation?

Zech snorts. "Yeah? After New Year's Eve, you can't talk." But he mouths "sorry" at the statue before rolling out of bed and grabbing his pants.

117

I let off the parking brake, then spin the wheel and press the accelerator, sending the 'Vi roaring up a steep slope and Zech tumbling back into his bed, headfirst.

"Isaiah!"

"Why don't you just sleep with your pants on like any sane hunter?"

"I like a bit of ventilation, cub."

"Oh, just get them on before you scare all the city-ladies." Cub, indeed. At twenty-one, he's only three years older than me.

At the reminder of the potentially dire situation we face, Zech lies on his back with his legs in the air and manages to wriggle into the pants, despite the fact that I'm driving at break-neck speed up the slope and down into the next valley. Then he grabs the Intercar mic. "What's the place called?"

"Er, Green Meadows or something, I think."

"Hello, Green Meadows Resort or whatever you are, this is the Wilson HabVi, what is your situation?"

Nothing but static. The resort's always stuffed full of noisy cityfolk and we've never been inside. We shot a wild edmontosaur within sight of their fence, once, and some manager fellow rushed out in a truck and begged us to take it away and *butcher it somewhere else*, shoving a wad of cash into Zech's hand before we could point out that obviously we were going to pull it *inside* the 'Vi first. Butchering carcasses near resorts

118

could be a nice little earner, clearly, but it feels too like extortion—kinda would be, I guess—so we've kept our distance since then.

Once we're over the next rise, Zech tries again. "Hello, Green Meadows Resort or whatever the name, this is the Wilson HabVi, what is your situation?"

"HabVi? Did you say *HabVi?*" The hysterical voice blasts from our speakers, making Zech turn them down quickly. "Are you hunters?"

"Yeah, we're hunters. What's the problem?"

"T. rex. There's a *T. rex*. It came straight through the electric fence; now it's wandering around, it's *roaring!*"

Zech rolls his eyes at me. Yeah, the poor beast's probably feeling well singed. "Roaring, huh? Is it doing anything else?" One singed rex looks fearsome but is unlikely to cause much trouble unless someone decides to run under its nose. "Did you get everyone inside?"

"How? Raptors came through the breach almost at once. They're everywhere. I keep broadcasting for people to *stay inside*, but every time the rex goes near a chalet someone panics and tries to run. The raptors— they're *eating* them."

No smile on Zech's face now. A resort full of helpless cityfolk, children too, no doubt...and raptors. "*Make* people stay inside," he snarls. "The rex is unlikely to try and get into a building, unless there's somewhere with a whole lotta food. And if your chalets are built to regulation, it'll take the raptors ages to breach one. So *make them stay inside!*"

"They're not listening to me..."

"Who are you, anyway? Can I speak to the senior fence guard?"

"I *am* the fence guard. I'd just come out to do the morning check when the rex..."

Zech huffs. The guy on the end of the Intercar doesn't seem very effective, for a fence guard. "Has anyone taken shelter in the dining room, kitchen, or food storage areas?"

"I don't know. I'm in the fence control booth."

"Get over there and check, then just drive back and forth and calm everyone down until we get there."

"I can't go *out*. There're raptors everywhere! I can't get to my vehicle."

Zech clenches his teeth. Yeah, he should've parked his vehicle closer, shouldn't he? Incompetent, for sure. "Fine, put some steel into your voice and do it all via intercom. *Explain* it to them. Don't run from the Rex. The Rex is not the danger. The danger is the raptors. So they must stay inside. Help is on the way. Make them stay put."

"I'll try. But they're not listening —"

"We'll be there soon."

120

Zech cuts the connection and dumps the mic back into its cradle. "Fence guard? I wouldn't want him guarding a *nursery*."

"I guess the rejects from the SPARK Brigade have to work somewhere." Only the best are accepted by the elite force that guards and maintains the huge city fences; small private settlements like the resort hire their own.

"Just put your foot down, Isaiah."

"What does it look like I'm doing, Zechariah?"

I let the huge vehicle drift across a wide curve of gravel, accelerating again as we begin to straighten out. In fact, I keep the accelerator hard down, despite the fact that we're tearing up the sod and leaving an ugly brown trail.

Zech slips into a t-shirt and sweater and has just thrown his ammo sash on when we top another rise.

"There it is, Zech."

Zech grabs the binos from a torn door pouch and focuses on the extensive settlement ahead. Extensive compared to the usual isolated farm, anyway. Rows of little chalets spread over the side of another gentle hill, with some bigger buildings at the summit. Manicured grounds down the back, I recall, and some more chalets.

A large shape moves, just visible over some of the chalets near the top, a stroppy roar carrying to our external mics.

"There's the rex." Zech's finger moves on the wheel of the binos. "Looks okay from here. Probably more shaken than anything. It's a juvenile male."

"What else would it be?"

"A juvenile female?"

"Not as often." But it's always a juvenile, that's for sure. Older rex know to stay away from electricity. If we can get this one out of there without killing it, it will know too. Which means getting it out alive is the highly preferred option. Otherwise the Dinosaur Activity and Population department (or DAPdep, as most people call it) will have to let another one hatch out—something's got to maintain a stable herbi'saur population, after all—and this will probably happen all over again, somewhere else, sooner than it need.

"What's the plan, Zech? Can you see the breach? Is it this side?"

Just the two of us to deal with a rex, at least one pack of raptors, and...how big a hole in the fence?

Zech scans the fence as we roar downhill like an armored juggernaut with massive wheels and huge tires. A rusty armored juggernaut.

"Ah, got it. Eight o'clock position. Looks like...hmm, from here I'd say a total breach, but no dragging to speak of."

Total breach, so the fence strands are actually

122

broken right in two, but they haven't been dragged far out of position, so it's a fairly small, clean hole. It could be worse. Could be better, too, since a partial breach—with electrified wires still lying across the hole—would help keep the raptors out.

"Raptor count?"

"I've spotted Dakotaraptors and Utahraptors already, so at least two packs. And I think I mighta seen a velociraptor tail, but I couldn't swear to that one."

"*Three packs?*" I can't help shooting Saint Des a reproachful look. Is this my comeuppance for New Year? "This is going to be a fun day."

Zech grunts agreement. "First off, we're going to quickly drive up and down between all those chalets, looking big and mean and broadcasting that the hunters are here now so everything's fine; they just need to stay indoors until we've dealt with the situation."

I can't help snorting slightly at that, but still. The most urgent thing is to calm people down enough that they stop feeding themselves to the raptors.

"Then we'll figure out how to get the rex out. Then fix the fence. Then it's just a raptor hunt."

"Oh joy." *Yeah, we're going to need your help today, Saint Des.* Saint Desmond the Hermit—who lived alone in a cave for twenty years without being eaten by any of the local raptor packs—has been the staunch patron saint of hunters and all those who live unSPARKed—outside an electric fence—ever since he was canonized, shortly after Zech and I were born. If he's got our back, we'll be fine.

"Gate, Zech?" Fighting to keep the heavy vehicle on course, I don't want to mess with the Intercar myself.

"Resort, this is the HabVi, please open your gate."

"Oh, thank God! You're here!"

The outer gate slides open ahead of us. Once we're inside the gate compound, I slow to a crawl until the outer gate has swooshed shut and the inner one opened. Through we go.

I drive straight for the chalets but stare at the fence control booth near the gate as we pass—and at the vehicle parked right outside. What's the guy playing at, staying in there?

"What's your intercom frequency?" Zech asks the guard, his voice tight.

"Er...dunno."

Zech growls, his hand tightening around the mic. "Fine, patch me through!" He gives the guard a moment to fumble with his equipment as I head for the road between the first two rows of chalets, then demands, "Ready?"

"Uh, yeah."

Zech breathes out deeply, letting his frustration with the guard go, and speaks calmly and authoritatively. "Resort guests, this is the Wilson HabVi, we are taking charge of this situation. Please stay indoors until further notice. If the Rex approaches your location, remain inside and it will walk on by. Raptors are loose in the resort, so under no circumstances go outside until further notice. Keep all doors and windows closed at all times. Resort guests, this is the Wilson HabVi..."

As I drive up and down the rows Zech keeps up his patter, sounding tough and chilled out, if not outright bored, just the way old Mister Wilson used to do it when we were younger. "Nothing calms panicked cityfolk like someone who's bored by a T. rex," he used to say. People wave from windows, faces naked with relief but no surprise, so the chalet's intercom system must be transmitting the message.

As we move higher up the hill, I slow down, not wanting to come up on the rex by accident. Zech, leaving a recording on loop setting, goes up to our observation turret for a better view. His rifle barks now and then as he picks off the odd raptor that doesn't zip out of sight fast enough. There's a risk the noise of gun and engines will attract the rex's attention, but they tend to hunt more by sight—movement, specifically. Thanks to something or other back when the foolish

125

scientists first bred them—arrogantly assuming they, like the rest of their "restorations," would never escape—rex don't identify static objects as prey.

Crack, goes Zech's rifle again.

"Yeah, there's velociraptors, for sure." We've both slipped our earpieces in so we can talk to one another easily. "One less, now."

I sigh. "Great."

I glance at the dashboard screen, which displays the feed from the forward pointing turret-top camera. The rex isn't that far ahead, now, still stamping and roaring angrily, so far paying us no heed, but if we get too close it might get interested since we're a moving object and we're taller than the chalets. At about fourteen feet tall, the juvenile can see over them too. "Zech, I'd better cut around it now so we can do the other side of the hill."

"Yep."

I turn right, trying to picture the gentle curves of the lines of chalets and plot a course that will take us clear of Rexie. Everywhere we drive up here, frightened faces peer from chalet windows and feathery raptor tails whisk away around corners. Who in their right mind would run outside just now? But they do. Too scared of the rex to realize the greater danger.

"Isaiah, stop." Zech's voice comes sharply and the

automated message playing into the Intercar mic cuts off as he silences it from the turret console above.

I ease us to a halt at once, glancing at the screen again as I cut the engine. The rex isn't in view on that cam but—a roar nearby—yes, it's moving closer to us. Coming to check us out? We'll have to wait for it to wander off again.

"Oh *outage, outage*..." Zech's soft, horrified whisper makes all the hair on the back of my neck stand up.

There... A little girl stumbles from between two chalets, her face screwed up in absolute, silent terror. Those thudding footsteps speed up abruptly, a smashing sound in the distance as the rex pushes past something. It glimpsed her, and it's coming. I've jerked the door open and swung down into the fresh morning air before I can even think. "Zech, cover me."

"Isaiah, no!"

I dart on an interception course. Before I can reach the tottering girl, a dark-clad human shape dashes from between the same two chalets, clearly in pursuit, and snatches her up.

"Quick, into the 'Vi!" I beckon as the man turns. He takes two steps towards me—

"Freeze!" Zech's voice in my ear is soft—and iron.

My hand flies up towards the man, palm flat. *"Stay still!"* I barely murmur it, but I mouth it *very* clearly.

The man skids to a halt as those heavy footfalls

grow louder—the only movement he makes is to fold both halves of his unzipped jacket over the child, enveloping her completely, and murmur something to her. Then he stands absolutely still, though the blood drains from his dark, dark skin, leaving it slightly grey-tinged.

From the slight *chink* sounds coming from my earpiece, Zech is swopping his rifle for the Rex gun, which he took up there with him though he was really hoping not to have to use it. But he shouldn't need it. Not if we just stand still.

I maintain eye contact with the man as the ground shakes under our feet and the rex appears around the chalet just behind him, its head swiveling as it searches for that flash of un-raptor-like movement. Not that the rex won't make do with raptor, if one comes too close, so we don't need to worry about those feathered killers until it clears off.

Keeping my face calm and relaxed, I study the man to take my mind off the approaching carni'saur. Dressed all in black, he looks several years older than Zech, mid-twenties, his tightly curling black hair close-cropped. Hmm, just visible over the jacket-wrapped little girl is a clerical collar. That's why he's all in black; he's a priest.

We're standing close enough together that I can see the sweat on his face, his wide pupils... I go back to meeting his gaze and trying to look unconcerned. Something as tiny as eye contact can make a huge difference to someone trying not to break and run. Makes them feel they're not alone, and people can endure all manner of things if only they aren't alone. Even cityfolk.

Thud. Thud. Thud. The rex comes closer, still looking around, nostrils flaring. I'm not wearing any ScentBlocker and for sure the other two aren't. If we stood in the middle of a field, that would be a big problem. But right here, in this human place surrounded by human scents, we won't stand out. *Right, Saint Des?*

The rex's head comes down, sniffing the front of the 'Vi, feet away from me, its distinctive carni'saur smell reaching my nostrils. A few scorch marks mar its otherwise smooth, healthy hide, and it's already growing quite a fine greenish-red display crest on top of its head, the only feathers retained by adult rex. From the way the priest's eyes widen, he's getting a good look at the beast. I try to hold his gaze, but he shuts his eyes tight. Praying, I guess. He still doesn't move, so that's fine.

Just don't let the little girl make a sound... Thank God he covered her head so she couldn't see. He's smart, for a city-man. Mebbe he can see Zech in the turret, pointing the rex gun. That should make him feel better, though if he knew how fast a rex can move when it feels like it...

Well. When the rex moves its head right close to me, sniffing, I add a few prayers of my own to his. I'm awfully tempted to shut my eyes as well, but I force myself to keep them open, taking in the details of a magnificent young animal I would never usually see so close-up. Though this is getting a little too close. Reeking rex breath overpowers every other scent. Sweat trickles down my forehead... The rex sniffs. Okay, *way* too close. If it sticks out that barely-mobile tongue and licks me, it'll *know* I'm prey...

Get BREACH! from your favorite retailer today!

ABOUT THE AUTHOR

Corinna Turner has been writing since she was fourteen and likes strong protagonists with plenty of integrity. Although she spends as much time as possible writing, she cannot keep up with the flow of ideas, for which she offers thanks—and occasional grumbles!—to the Holy Spirit. She is the author of over twenty-five books, including the Carnegie Medal Nominated I Am Margaret series, and her work has been translated into four languages. She was awarded the St. Katherine Drexel award in 2022.

She is a Lay Dominican with an MA in English from Oxford University and lives in the UK. She is a member of a number of organizations, including the Society of Authors, Catholic Teen Books, Catholic Reads, the Angelic Warfare Confraternity, and the Sodality of the Blessed Sacrament. She used to have a Giant African Land Snail, Peter, with a 6½" long shell, but now makes do with a cactus and a campervan.

Get in touch with Corinna...

Facebook: Corinna Turner

Twitter: @CorinnaTAuthor

Don't forget to sign up for

NEWS
&
FREE SHORT STORIES
at:

www.UnSeenBooks.com

All Free/Exclusive content subject to availability.

Made in United States
Troutdale, OR
02/21/2024

17856773R00083